I0749196

JOSEPHINE
THE OUTLAW KING

JEANNETTE LOUISE KANTZALIS

NeoPoiesis Press, LLC

NeoPoiesis Press
P.O. Box 38037
Houston, TX 77238-8037

www.neopoiesispress.com

Copyright © 2012 by Jeannette Kantzalis

All rights reserved. No part of this book may be used or reproduced in any manner whatsoever without express written permission from the publisher except in the case of brief quotations embodied in critical articles and reviews.

Josephine the Outlaw King by Jeannette Louise Kantzalis
ISBN 978-0-9832747-6-6 (hardback : alk. paper)
1. Fiction: Crime. I. Kantzalis, Josephine

Edited by Jeff Vintar and Yolanda Gillies
Printed in the United States of America.

First Edition

For Aron, Theodore and Flynn.
There's no reason to do anything
without you.
This book is dedicated to you.

To my Mom and Dad. You've supported me every single day of my life,
no matter what the crazy scheme.
There aren't enough "thank you's" in the world to say how grateful I am to both of you for your love and sacrifice.

I love you.

A special thanks to
Jeff Vintar and Yolanda Gillies.

You two are such troublemakers! If it weren't for you I would've never considered writing a book. Because of your generosity, expertise and talent, I actually did it.

And last but not least a very special thanks to Neil McCrea, Dale Winslow and Erin Badough.

Neil, you're such a big part of this novel. Thanks so much for your support, help, knowledge and unflappable belief that I could actually do this. I can't tell you how much it means to me.

Dale and Erin, thank you so much for believing in me and helping me to make this dream come true.

Contents

SOMEBODY WAITS FOR YOU.

Chapter 1

The Truth About Josephine Lilliwhite

He left her bleeding on a gray gravel rough tongue of a road. Good and dead, he thought. He could jerk away now. He could go on. He took the giant steps towards her, the kind that can only be stomped out by a selfish beast. With Josephine dead, he felt fully born, big and birthed.

Finally, she was stone still, all of her dark-red life soaking into the sand. He thought her a lovely, muddy pie now. He cocked his head sideways, framing her every which way. Yeah, just right, he mused. He always thought she should've remained a picture, the kind you see hanging still and clear across a smoke-blurred room. Click.

But she had turned and looked back at him that sweltering summer night, hadn't she? She had animated. She had faced him and she had surely smiled. His head exploded, his heart popped open and his blood heated and thinned.

Josephine was just too much for him when she moved.

That's why he brought the gun.

He'd heard she was swelling. It had been a little over a year since she left him unexpectedly while his mind had his back to her. He'd always figured she'd still be there when he wasn't too busy thinking about himself.

The rumor of another man was almost too much for him and the chatty crows pecked and chirped the story of a truly happy Josephine. His ears stung from too many shardlike beaks stabbing his drums with the unbearable news of her life without him. A good and tender one at that.

They cawed that Josephine was filled. Their shrieking screamed of a new life, a new man and another child.

A son.

Her second.

His one true accomplishment in this life, bested. Having a child with Josephine was the only worthy thing he'd ever done, the only thing he'd ever given her that she really, truly wanted.

Now another has mirrored his great feat!

He didn't want to believe it. He needed liars now more than ever.

But Josephine's pregnant saunter deemed the ratty flock truthful, and she swayed with a full glow that she wore proudly to their meeting. Her silhouette against the desert sky made him sick and it made him mad. She was asking for it.

Had she really believed he was calling to congratulate her? Did she really think he was okay with her leaving him behind? He was not okay. No, he was very, very rough.

This intruder's seed had made Josephine stupid, he thought.

But Josephine thought differently.

This good man had made her sharp. He had whittled away the dullness and buffed her bright. He was her divine and personal savior.

He was her Saint.

You see, this man had done the impossible: He'd made her hopeful.

Hope could be such a dangerous thing when it's planted in the heart of an amateur like Josephine. She had indeed deprived herself the luxury of wishing her entire life and the introduction of possibility had proven to be an intoxicating handshake.

Josephine opened her arms and gave the beast a sweet embrace. The feel of Josephine, her scent and her swell were more than he could bear.

The time had come to end this ridiculous and humiliating folly.

He inhaled strength and exhaled lead as the barrel spit out the purposeful pellet.

Lying there wetting and puddling into the sparkling grains, Josephine made the decision not to empty out. She learned right then and there how to statue. She slowed it all down, the beat, the bleeding, the motion. She locked herself in the pose he'd snapped of her years before.

Josephine made a promise as the pain spun out in rings from the bullet hole: She would take to rising every morning and she'd burst with breath every new day.

This new death would be the coronation, the crowning of her new life.

Josephine the Outlaw King would now reign.

Her mind was clear now and for the first time in a long while she knew exactly what she must do to walk away from this unfortunate attempt at her ending.

If he found out she still took to the selfish habit of rising, he would surely be back to finish this gunpowder bake.

Real snakelike is how he'd do it. He'd finish her off and put a new back on. A faster one no doubt, a real reptilian wrapper. Yeah, that's how his scales slid and they'd leave sticky yellow stains all over the alleys and floors, all over his well-known strangers and unknown friends.

She possumed perfectly and let the madness spill out and stain what was supposed to have been an agreeable, amicable truce.

Don't think he didn't have that moment, the one where he'd walk back to her pale body encased in that soft, steely white.

Don't think he didn't stop and stand over her, watching it all seep out.

Don't think he didn't peek through the soft black strands striping her face to see if the hazel eyes still looked away from him now.

Looking down on Josephine made him feel a great conquering had occurred. The taming of something fierce and something very wild had snapped from his whip.

Then he noticed something in her stopped expression that made him shiver.

The stretched and glassy mask that now lay across Josephine's once-trusting face reflected a new image of a thing he'd never had the guts to gander. Gone was the face of a dark hero, the heroic companion of a shy and lonely girl. In her eyes he saw the vile and cowardly creature he'd become.

A Monster.

Her Monster. Josephine had re-created him in her final gaze to appear as he really was and how he'd always be. This was all her fault. His brain made the necessary twists, in and out and backwards through the lying loop creating a knot of rationalization that couldn't be untangled or untied.

He looked down on her again.

She was so lovely, so sweet, even in her death.

Don't think he didn't start to breathe heavy.

Don’t think he didn’t get hard.

Don't think he didn't think it.

Don't think he didn't do it.

He pushed and pumped past the swollen belly of Josephine, past her bright and shiny future. Take that and that and that, he huffed.

He slithered it all back home, shrunk and spent, all natural like, saddling whatever metal he’d stolen to lure her out there.

Josephine waited the longest hour until The Monster laid his guilty tracks.

After no stir dusted up around her, Josephine dared to peek out. The blood was more than the gash and she couldn't feel it anymore.

And her baby did kick. Her heart did beat. Nothing was as still as The Monster had thought.

She stumbled. You know what it looked like, gripping her belly and gently whispering to that baby, “Everything’s going to be all right. Mama will take care of you. I'll beat double, one for me, one for you, my baby boy. You rest.”

She made stuttered strides all up that dirty sugar. It seemed like the mounds would never end; there weren't any outlines.

Finally she found the iron ride, that 1964 Lincoln Continental, the slickest suicide machine ever to slide out and off of the great American working-class line.

Black on black, pure leather and steel. My god, it was handsome.

It was The Saint's.

She gripped the old chromie and made a squeeze she didn't know she had in her. She filled the seat and squared away the key.

It struck up like it had just come off the line, it did. It bore such a heavy, it even stifled its own rumble. That seasoned machine sucked the oil-soaked asphalt dry as she drove the rumbling back roads toward the memory of a hospital she hoped she hadn't simply imagined. Finally, Josephine saw the big, block red letters of EMERGENCY. As she pulled in, the faint darkened the inside of her dizzy and she passed out.

She awoke to so much bright white. It was just everywhere.

She was now an anonymous thing in a sterile bed, a quiet and unknown being, unfamiliar to even herself.

She felt her flattened middle and shot up wildly just as the nurse brought her the child.

Life got bigger for Josephine and she multiplied to three that Thursday night, both wounds patched, baby boy and mama healthy and ready. They had to be. They'd be going back for his brother as soon as she dressed.

She knew the hissy spit of the news would reach The Saint and he'd be forced to believe the black-and-white, the talking heads and the liquid relatives. He'll try so hard to kill back that mourning. He'll fail. He'll take to the out and try to pull his Josephine back in.

He'll hope the hardest hope that she still had enough pints to float her back home, back to him, back to their love and their life that had barely started.

For the first time in her lonely history, somebody waited for her.

Somebody waited for Josephine.

As she fed her newborn prince, she plotted the steps toward her return. Josephine now owned the courage to take back her kingdom, to fight for what was rightfully hers. For the first time in her life she knew exactly what she wanted and how she was going to get it.

Josephine heard the soft back-and-forth footfall of the busy-bee nurses and interns in the hall outside of her room.

One set of stomps halted their shuffle right in front of her door. The slender shadow shot out from under the crack and lay across the speckled linoleum.

Josephine turned to steel and shielded her newborn as the door swung slowly inward.

Her fear turned to relief and back to fear again as the officer introduced himself.

“I’m Detective Bullock, ma’am. I’ve got a couple of questions, if that’s okay with you? I know you’ve just been through some kinda hell but I need to get some facts straight so I can catch the person or persons who did this. Would that be alright with you, ma’am?”

Josephine knew this was coming. She had to think of something quick before this neon arrow carelessly blinked her whereabouts to The Monster. She nodded reluctantly.

Detective Dennis Bullock was pure Inland Empire, born and raised, Josephine could see that. He wouldn’t dig too deep now. No, he’d wait until he could see all the way down before jumping in. Josephine tried her hardest to darken her waters, mimicking a neverending infinite.

He wanted to know the sights, the sounds and the speeches that came before, during and after.

Josephine answered as if she were blind, deaf and dumb. She told him she didn't see or hear anybody. She said she couldn't remember screaming or anything else that happened after the bang. She didn't know when or how she got there, she only knew she had a brand new baby boy to take care of and she was going to make sure he was safe.

He believed nothing but the last sentence. This was a woman who knew exactly what she was dealing with and was determined to handle it on her own.

Josephine blinked slowly and rubbed her eyes.

"I'm tired Detective. Can't we finish this tomorrow?"

Bullock nodded sympathetically. He tucked his pen and pad into his shirt pocket and said he'd be back in the early afternoon.

The name she gave the nurses was surely a fake. She was smart enough to leave no trail, and he didn't blame her for lying.

It didn't matter. He knew how to get what he needed.

He stepped out into the hallway and shook his head. He knew she'd be gone by morning. He hated the deflated feeling of being utterly powerless but there's no changing the made-up mind of a woman undone.

Josephine stroked the baby's cheek, gently rocking him while he slept. This sweet baby didn't know how dangerous their world had become. She placed him in the crib and leaned back into the crisp pillowcase.

Josephine felt quite heavy and quite done.

As the detective walked through the hospital parking lot, he tried to shake the image of the tiny woman melting into the giant bed. He imagined her sinking under the weight of her new iron reserve as it coated her once light and tender nerves.

He knew her type. He had loved one just like her.

They met in high school. Tracy was the loudest cheerleader at Fontana High. Bullock fell for her before the first pom-pom dropped, he did. They married as soon as they graduated and had three little girls, all redheads, just like their mother.

He adored his women. They gave him a life he never knew existed, a love he never dared believe in, and Tracy was the center of it all.

She was taken from him on a Thursday night two summers ago. Someone, or rather, some "thing", had stolen her, taken her deep inside a dull and painful hell. The fiend didn't even have the decency to do it quickly. No, he fumbled and dragged it out with a thick blade making a mess of the perfect throat that used to belt to eleven proudly at every game.

As Bullock slid onto the tattered blue bench of his trusty Ford pick-up, he took a deep breath and blinked away the hot tears of frustration. He'd never come close to finding Tracy's killer and he was going to have a hell of a time finding who, or what did this to that petite brunette in Room 102.

"There must be somebody back home who waits for you," he muttered. He twisted the key and revved his rumbler back home, back to his three beautiful daughters. He'd leave his sadness in the rusted cab for now like he did every night before he stepped through the door that used to be filled with four fiery redheads.

Josephine knew she couldn't stay much longer. Someone would connect the crimson dots soon enough. She'd stay in the shadows until she could figure out just what it was she needed to do out in the light. She wasn't too proud to admit she didn't have a plan, but her instincts were sharper than razor blades now.

She'd unwrap the shiny sharps as needed. She'd trust in their edge for the first time in her life, believing it her best weapon against the sins that faced her.

Through a well-earned and achingly deep breath, Josephine whispered to no one, “You can’t stop me. Bullets ain’t brakes.”

Chapter 2

That's Your Josephine

Miss Josephine was a fine figure of a woman, a real-life simple fancy thing. She was like one of those gals drawn and pictured all the time in all sorts of postures and poses. She had that faraway look of a time gone by.

You know the kind of gal, the satisfying sort of stapled date-keeper that ends up hanging in the garage because she's not allowed to hang in the house. It's not like she could actually curve and slither right off the gloss into their scratchy marital bed, but something in her longing look betrayed her true nature. Maybe the fanning-the-flames gaze of a dreamer can look like a threatening stare to souls who'd given up on any kind of sweetness long ago.

That's the plight of a real-life look-upon.

Not to worry, a muse knows her place. Let her be pinned proudly and prominently on the wall of some suburban stucco hotbox that houses the dreamer and his wheels. They'll share the late part of the night, the part he has to fight for sometimes. He'll polish some kind of steel and lean on the rod that'll rip him right out of there.

And he'll imagine a woman just like our Josephine right beside him.

But could he imagine the regal swagger that stomped and clipped quiet in her worn boots, those square-toed, black-strapped engineer jobbers she kept cobbling?

Did he know that beneath those clomps slipped easily onto her seven and a half's were some ready-set tens varnished her signature crimson?

Her sizes and colors, letters and numbers, they all seemed to matter somehow.

There were the Levi's, always the hard-to-find 524s. She must've had a dozen pairs, all in different stages of thread death.

She'd top it all off with a basic tee, boy's medium. She'd sack a pack of three for ten dollars at her local JCPenney's. Josephine favored a fresh and new one quite often so she kept a drawer filled with some never-worns, blue-white and ready for a good stretch.

This was the uniform of our Outlaw King.

Her skin was another necessary accessory and it matched everything. Pale-pale it was, a complementary contrast to her silky, brown-black Hayworth waves.

Josephine's soldier of a ride had kept quite well over the years and it always snapped back, saluting and reporting for duty no matter how hard the battle, no matter how awful the war.

Even after both of her bigheaded baby boys laid their screaming skids on this planet, not a tread mark can be seen on our Mama Royale, although her steely white did show some wear from the daytime.

The spectacular glare of the Southern California sun she was born under had sprinkled soft, vulnerable freckles on her out in the open parts. It threw her sometimes, looking down on the stormy hands changing the diaper of her springtime newborn. It was such a lucky and lovely contrast.

The full-grown, full-blown, creased and softened Majesty bore both princes in her later half. Her life before them was all prep. All her "why" worry turned into "oh" and "ah yes" nods.

Everything suddenly made sense when the boys began their beating.

Everything.

Still, Josephine had no idea she was such an inky blue blood. The dusty land that laid course through mountains, lakes and dunes struggling to cast her out was indeed her land. The natural fights that seemed to find her weren't started to end the girl nor were they arranged to smash her face in the dirt for the entertainment of the invited. The fall of the punch was supposed to force an inhale, to make the reluctant royal catch and recognize the perfume of her birthright. The bashings were merely fate's fingers poking shocking jolts into Josephine's tender spine trying to jump-start the woman that would be King.

But as a child, Josephine never knew her worth. She quite frankly thought the blows were meant to keep her down, to show her where she truly belonged. Her birth was some sort of lustful mistake most likely, some sort of angelic, clerical error of sorts. She came to feel she'd fallen through the cracks and had somehow landed in the place of a true and deserving soul. Josephine bore the weight of a thief's guilt and built strange strength because of it.

Sometimes, that same little girl glared out from behind the faded browns of a forgotten woman. They had started off Greek, you know, like her father's, dark like some foreign chocolate. Add some of the creamy French, ice-blue lady stuff her mother sported and boom–they flooded hazel in a frenzy.

Funny things, the folks. Still fighting through her blood, scrapping for some common thread to connect them to this creature. They looked long and hard for anything of theirs they could recognize. Then what did that Josephine child go and do? She mixed all of their things together until she resembled nothing they could relate to.

She churned the calm and the temper together to make a buttery, righteous anger. She let the soft lay over the steel, melding into a fine, new structure.
She became unrecognizable to her parents and they felt even farther from her as she grew, knowing nothing of this new and strange animal, their animal. She was their truest mix, their finest gesture but they couldn't get past the fact that she looked like she came from someone or something else.

Although Josephine's sons both favored their fathers, she never felt them far from her. They shared her knowing eye, they did.

The shape flashed daddy, the color borrowed grandma's blue, but their steady gaze was all Josephine. Their stance and stomp was most definitely Mama, Mama, Mama.

Off into the ruddiness Josephine would have to go, striking through the sand-and-sky sandwich toward the lowest piece of her desert, the grittiest part of her kingdom. It was the place she'd have to call home for a little while.

Two stacked hearts all asway, one right side up, one upside down.

Her hourglass turning over and over, the grains never running out, our Josephine was indeed timeless,

time filled,
time-tested and
true.

That's a woman, all right.

That's your Josephine.

Chapter 3

Josephine on the Back of the '64 Suicide Machine

That meeting wasn't a meeting at all, now was it? It was some kind of bumbled ambush. Not so fair, Monster, and not so fast. Josephine paced it back and forth, pounding out her signature black-boot stomp.

He had finally frightened her. His scare changed her cells, moved her DNA all around. That shot shook her delicate bones and rearranged them. She changed shape with this newfound skeleton right before her very own eyes.

Would The Saint still recognize her?

Josephine didn't want to think about the battle she had to face and she made a decision not to revisit that dark, red and loud scene until she was strong enough. For now, she'd leave that stop off her route.

Since she was twelve, she'd been taking nightly head trips, visiting all of her past mistakes. She'd go over the details of every failure she'd ever committed and she'd administer a flogging any bitter nun would be proud of. It felt good knowing the exact berate to make your heart hurt like that, to make you ashamed of breathing, taking in air you're not worthy of whiffing.

Josephine couldn't stifle the how-dare-you's and the how-could-you's howling and hollering inside her reshaped skull. She didn't like this kind of mad, no ma'am. She found the fresh white layer under the one he'd scraped away so ticklish and vulnerable.

Josephine didn't wear this skin well at all.

She warmed her hands and rubbed her limbs, toughening them to touch.

She tried to keep the shivery bumps of memories calm while she contemplated her first, most important battle: the taking back of Sun Son.

Her worry over him almost drowned her. She'd given herself minutes to get a steady swagger and stroke going again and she granted herself some tiny hours to plan his retrieval, committing to the unforgiving swing of the row that crashed ahead. She'd have to make it back from that very angry sea with everyone intact, or die trying.

Her body was still healing from the birth of her little Moonface. She felt the murky cloud of tired swimming through her thickness. Top that with a healing hole from a slightly missed bullet and you've got a truly fatigued fighter.

Let it be a known and planned battle next time, my dear Monster. And let the toll of the last surprise be laid on your very own greasy wealth of a gushing belly.

She threatened low like she had his ear and had it close. Such an angry wish, sour tasting like skunky fear-metallic. She slumped next to the sweetest baby sleeping like everything was going to be all right. His perfect little angel sigh made Josephine weep. Finally.

She sobbed softly until she was dry, and then it was done.

She couldn't afford the luxury of breaking.

That temper of hers was another deep pocket ripper. It costs about a million minutes for such impatience and insecurity. A warrior's wage was never enough; she'd need a king's ransom to cover that debt of time.

She set out on a Thursday. She was hardening quick and fitting into the suit of armor just fine. She filled the Lincoln with baby and mama and set out to overflow it with her first-born.

She knew where he was. She always knew where he was.

The Monster had seen fit to drop him off with the most careless caretaker, his soulless junkie of a mother.

Prescribed, she claimed over and over, prescribed and very much needed for the endless pain she had to endure. So much more than anybody else in this life, she'd wail. She needed every single milligram, she did. Josephine snarled with the memory.

Just giving that woman a momentary thought made Josephine's jaw set hard in its grind and she kept the rest of her thoughts focused on the baby behind her and the glaring empty spot between them.

She knew this woman well. She'd been her housekeeper for a while, and the messes this troll could achieve were uncleanable.

The wretched thing had a revolving system of victims that encircled her. It made it even more difficult to keep her house in order. These poor planets were stuck in her swirling torrents of woe and bad luck. Josephine never understood the gravity this woman owned because she never felt the pull of it herself.

She often witnessed The Thing pop the inevitable trip over an unseen crack. Josephine marveled at the grace of it and her steady shuffle off, wearing pajamas two sizes too big. The Thing never dressed to go out.

Josephine had jumped and reared up so many times at the slam of her bedroom door because somebody had disobeyed an imagined order. She hated that Thing's childishness and she never entertained it. This made for an interesting dynamic. The Thing suckled Josephine like a mother.

This woman was a masterpiece, a symphony of self-pity, self-loathing and unabashed viciousness. Bing, bang, boom went her band of silly whining and the notes grew shriller with each ignored measure.

But it wasn't Josephine who had seen her at her worst. It was her son, The Monster. This was the core of his problem and now it seemed a central part of The Thing's predicament as well.

Josephine was dead sure of what she was going to do, and she'd end what should never have been started.

The blade was sleeping against her deflated belly, between the Levi's and the softest skin possible. It soaked up her heat. Good thing. She felt like she was going to burst into flames and the steel sinks quicker when warmed.

She was so ready to put that mean Thing down, cease her supposed misery. Nobody waits for a ruiner like her, nobody.

Josephine pulled up the long driveway and checked her dear, sweet Moonface, sleeping new and deep.

Three loud pounds on the door would bring her. She'd stop her clock as soon as Son Sun was safe in the car. He wouldn't see a thing and he'd begin the task of being his brother's keeper right then and there.

The Thing split the entry and leaned out. She was more wasted along than the last time Josephine had come face to face with this goblin, more absent and hollow. Josephine always assumed she'd just go on and on, embalmed with forgotten deeds and plastic-wrapped with the fake expressions she'd memorized from old television shows.

The hag squinted and mumbled a name that wasn't Josephine's but instead that of Josephine's sister. Josephine was stunned that she remembered she even had a sister. The thing nodded as if to say, yeah, that's who you are.

"Come for the boy, finally? He's somewhere around here."

Josephine's heart bashed and slammed hard. If this creature had touched one golden hair on her son's royal head, she'd rip out a thousand of this Thing's wires and anything connected to the filthy tangle, including some of the rotting skull, and stuff it sideways through her shriveled heart.

Josephine dipped her head down and kept her eyes steady inside the creep's foggy blur.

She suddenly realized it after her own mad veil had cleared: This Thing could only see smudge. Her ears, they heard very little over the hiss.

She'd done herself too much damage, and it melted everybody into one being.

Josephine wasn't even there.

As far as The Thing was concerned, she never really was. She saw only herself, first, last, always. Her reflection in someone's eyes, that's what she searched for in a gaze.

The Thing was dying right in front of Josephine. It was the first, the only unselfish act this worn-out timepiece had ever ticked up for anybody. The job was done.

Josephine patted the blade subtly, tenderly. No work for you today.

Right on cue, the meteor rush that housed her first boy crashed into her legs with a good sound hug and a squeal. Josephine pulled him up into her arms and held him like he'd just been born. He was more hers now than he'd ever been.

She buried her head in his neck and swallowed tears, hers and his. She carried him to the car, and his smile was as wide as Josephine's.

Sun Son peeked into the back seat.

“Is that him, Mama? Is that our baby”?

Moonface beamed wide and open and the identical pairs of baby blues met for the first time. Smiles all around, smiles so badly needed, so desperately wanted. The brothers were now locked and loaded for life.

Josephine felt the first tingle of victory as she sped out and off, deep into the desert. The boys fell asleep within a few quick miles, safe and content, while she told them the first of many noble tales.

Josephine noticed the melody of her bedtime stories had changed. Foreboding, hopeful and true plucks were the only notes she had now. The heroes were two princes and Josephine warned them that their enemies looked like everybody and anybody only shinier. As the gilded ones slipped deep into their velvet, she imagined what their crowns would be made of. Not gold, no, not for them. The purest silver, white hot and light for their tiny blonde heads. They'd hold them high and know what they were born to do. Her weighted tin circle would not be theirs to bear. This was their Mama’s promise.

She sunk her foot deep into the gas pedal of that ‘64. The black dragon with its suicide wings always obliged the Outlaw King.

This bolt of borrowed and lucky thunder split open the gritty, hot wind. It felt like a forked tongue of breath in a way. Josephine hummed a song of the tallest nature. She grew with each mile, big enough to fight any and every ghoul army that threatened her mighty heart.

The royal fight for the greater good had begun.

Josephine wasn't tired. Sated by the flight, she supposed. Full of spark and flashing hope she sped on knowing he was out there celebrating her demise. She'd always protected him under her roof but that dwelling disintegrated a long time ago. The Monster's unshielded now and she knows all his prior cuts. She'd traced the scars with her very own fingertips and they pushed in soft and weak, they did.

She had taught The Monster everything he knows.

But she didn't teach him everything she knows.

That would be Josephine's extra fist in the fight for her kingdom.

Chapter 4

Josephine's Sun Son

Josephine's eight year old was golden and blue, tall and beautiful. "Sun Son" she'd call through a mama stern smile, "Sun Son, come here, boy!" He'd make a beeline, bounding at her all long-limbed like The Monster, straight hair swinging over his full brows. She'd look into him sometimes and think there are no bad recipes, no stale ingredients. All this little concoction needs is a proper chef and a sturdy, stainless place setting.

Josephine never spat a bad line or plucked a downing word to the tune of his father. Her eldest boy would only know that he housed the best of him, the best of both of them.

Josephine knew the good things about Sun Son's father before he endured the pummel of a twisted mother. That mother Thing took his trust and murdered it. It died clutching his conscience and his joy.

She let their son know his Da had been beaten by life and didn't have the weapons to fight back, the kind of weapons a mother does forge. She assured him that his very own Mama was pounding steel to the finest points for him, ready when he was.

She also made sure Sun Son knew he was loved big and loved clean. Josephine was good at that. She was very good at that. She punched through the expectations and pillowed him with unconditional kisses.

Josephine could and would raise only gentlemen.

And loving Sun Son was so very easy. Loving him made her happy. Loving him made her heart so big that it spilled over the sides, all over everything around them.

That boy, he did share Josephine's smile. Nice and neat squares pushing the inside of the full lips upward and out. Pink and lovely, plush pillows, and he used that mouth honestly. Well, most of the time he did. He would try the charming little boy lies every now and again. It would drop Josephine's head down to a scolding angle as she narrowed her eyes and warned without a word.

In Sun Son, what she had was a good thinker and an even greater laugher. He used those tools to twist Josephine back to "pleased" when she sported a troubled mask. He was a good boy to notice and a better son to care. He was indeed a prince.

The first-born prince of the Outlaw King.

Chapter 5

Josephine's Moonface

Josephine's newborn was moonfaced with a crown of blond curls. He had the blue eyes like his brother, and the two princes were psychic magnets in each other's presence. Brothers ever true in the grip of it all. Isn't that something? she'd muse.

And this baby, oh, he had a demanding pitch that he used for all sorts of things! He splashed out of Josephine with that hearty scream and it suited mama's strong ears just fine. He was alive and that yell reminded her of that happy fact every time he employed it.

That wide-open face was like a fried-egg moon on Sunday, and peaceful storms passed through him just like his Daddy Saint. Looking down on her baby was a study in longing. She hard-ached for his father but this baby made it a sweet kind of squeeze. He mixed in him all three. Isn't that something? she mused again.

Moonface inherited Josephine's independent streak and her whip-snap of a temper. That scream was the first sign of it. Impatience. That was Josephine's weakness.

It ran in the family, it did. It ran like spilled ink on foil, it did. Once the weighted liquid tipped that blood-related bottle, there was no stopping the stain. Mama Josephine had her work cut out for her with this little trinket. A job she looked forward to.

He wriggled and pushed his way out of those ever-present mama arms as soon as she let him think he had the strength to pull off such a feat. He'd swing his chub-chubs from side to side and grunt like a brute as if to say, I'm the boss! Indeed, child, indeed. A bit of his Daddy's English piece right there.

This baby had come through so much already that when he finally landed in Josephine's arms he felt so good. He felt right. He was so meant to be here.

With every kiss laid upon this child's lovely cap she whispered, "Hold on, just hold on." It became her wish, her hope, her prayer and her goal.

This baby boy, this newborn prince was indeed a royal, and now there were two.

Josephine's golden ones.

Chapter 6

Josephine's Saint Mattered in This World

It was still hard for Josephine to believe there was another woman that came before her in The Saint's life. It's not like he had handfuls of fingerprints denting his olive skin, but the evidence of another always leaves invisible scars. To Josephine, he always seemed too good for just anybody to touch.

That premier witness, that faux woman thing didn't love him. She couldn't see how he mattered in this world. That femme fugazi of an ex may have had him first but he was Josephine's last, her once and her for-all.

That curvy-come-first thing sensed his value. She whiffed him as he strode by, fresh off the aisle of her first wedding. Still gardenia-scented and drowning in tulle, she put herself back on the market with her veil freshly lifted and the kiss still wet on her lips.

She saw The Saint and felt the "single" tingling deep beneath her wedding corset.

Imagine that.

The Faux had always feared that such a man truly existed. The fable of a real one was almost too much for her senses. When he lifted his dark glance toward her she felt fairytale lucky that day. Trolls and witches be damned to hell, her knight in brand-new armor had finally arrived. She gave a shrug as she strode the silk runner and chalked it all up to unfortunate timing. She'd have it all fixed up before the cake was cut.

When he noticed her stare fixated deep he felt movie-star noticed. It was intoxicating.

He didn't know she was looking in the mirror of his eyes and my, my, didn't she look swell?

She knew everything right then and there.

She had a kind of a porn brilliance.

He was a young man.

She was a naked genius.

The Faux came to him with damage from a badly timed birth. Born too soon to a family not even close to being ready for a baby, let alone a baby girl. She was born when they were very busy. Busy fighting, busy stealing and very busy drinking.

The Faux was too much of a coward to address her parent's sins, so the wounds just sort of mutated into some very obvious scars and left her with a strange and ravenous hunger. She craved parts, any part, every part.

Hands that weren't too busy. She wanted them on her, in her, clapped together for her.

And eyes, she wanted pairs and pairs of them, the kind that never averted. She wanted all their gazes on her even when she wasn't there. She made naked movies to make it possible.

The Faux wanted mouths that didn't inquire. That didn't ask skin to cover up or legs to close.

She wanted faulty ears, a real selective pair of shells that could only hear kind and wonderfuls.

The Saint? He knew all of this and still he loved her. His heart was good. His soul was, too. He was all he should be and humble enough not to feel complete.

He was a young man.

She was a bone collector.

She was around the same age but she wore some kind of pre-old that dug see-through cracks so deep and sharp that they swallowed people up within two blocks of her.

She hid it with her own special pancake, and it worked most of the time.

He believed her when she said she'd jumped over the divides and survived; why wouldn't he?

She figured she'd get some of his sweet rub-off if she could at least have his name.

He gave it to her. Why wouldn't he?

He was a young man.

She was a title thief.

She took it. She took it and wore it big and bright when she met other men, armed with her bottomless, gaping hole.

That gash was unfillable, it was. She'd tossed diamonds down it, cash and bones. They landed with a hollow jingle jangle and disappeared past the darkness.

He was a young man.
She was an unwishing well.

She spoke his name loud and clear like it was her secret question to reveal.

And the answer? Well, it was never whispered to her. Not by The Saint, not by anybody. It was never shouted from his rooftop, either. The Fugazi still owned nothing that resembled a reply. She was left with the emptiest why and it made her angry.

The Saint was too good for her. She knew that. She knew that, and she never let on.

She lived in fear that somebody, anybody would find that out and lean into him with the truth.

They'd tell him, and she'd melt into matter.

He'd wade through her laughing and splashing in the lousy puddles.

She was sure of it.

She was wrong.

No, if there was even a softly bashing whisper, anything not matching the stroke of what he knew she could be, would be, why, he would've suddenly come down with the deaf sickness.

It's a special illness a loyal contracts when touched in the heart by a betraying germ.

The Faux feared her secret was impatient. She felt it pacing. It seeped out onto their sunset honeymoon. It swirled and whined shrill for years as he paid her angry debts, loving his duty while still loving her.

This made his worth even more bewildering to her. Her cheap started to wear through the shiny veneer. She knew she'd have to put herself on sale.

She knocked more off the original price each day.

His value soared as he floated on her known lies. He waited for her to believe what he believed: That she was indeed worth more. He was a young man.

She was the Blue Light Special.

You know, he didn't crumble when he learned of her sharing. He didn't melt fast under the red-hot flash of a misplaced Polaroid. He merely faded away from the ready film.

It was indeed her worst fear, and yet she had run to that ruin as fast as the golden ring could rumble and roll.

He was now a grown man.

She was fading fast.

It was his damage repaired that made him pulse. A boy who became a man by growing his heart big, growing his heart well, in spite of the big bad bully of life and he held that heart open against their closed and pounding fists.

The fighting only spread strong shoulders and sorted scrapping made for tender hands. It gave him generous ears and sincere actions, and it supplied him with the strength a man needs to go wise into this world.

She couldn't love him, that fake, faux thing.

She couldn't see how he mattered in this world.

She couldn't bear the weight of his worth.

But Josephine could.

She could see him, and as her first bit of good luck would have it, he could see her.

He saw her like it was a first, like she was his last, his always.

She was why he'd kept to standing straight up no matter how heavy the slam of the hammer.

Josephine could see him above all the backstage boys.

She was why he'd become strong and smoothed out. It was all for Josephine.

He was her man.

And Josephine was so his woman.

Chapter 7

The Monster and the Woman Who Would Be King

Before The Saint there was also a "somebody" in Josephine's life. When she met Sun Son's soon-to-be Da, he was just a belting boy, a loud and strutting thunderous thing that only wanted to be seen and heard. His instincts were childlike and he wished for the biggest and the best for himself. Nothing less would do.

Back then he didn't have a thirst for a gallon of girl, and the pint-sized serving of a woman called Josephine might be just enough feminine fill for the giant to swallow whole.

The Monster had sensed something overflowing the day they met but he tipped and poured her anyway. He knew her sacred heart pumped the good and strong blood of an ancient crown and he watched it lip his golden goblet with the first hello. The spill would leave a stain he could never make clean.

His future queen whisked by him and he inhaled the sweet cherry vanilla. A bunch of tomorrows with that scent, what a perfect little demand it made on the senses. He liked it. He liked her.

But Josephine wasn't a queen, not his, not anybody's. He was dead-on about the royal bloodline but he was never more wrong about anything than when he mistook her to be his second-in-command. That's not how it works in our Wildest West, no sir, not in our American Underground. Our titles here have no gender attached and neither do the tasks the throne requires.

Quite simply, our kings must fight for the greater good no matter what. The queen supports and facilitates the king. The king's crown bears all the responsibility and sets forth the plan of action. The king participates in every battle and sometimes is the war's only soldier fighting. The queen keeps all of the king's secrets and speaks his unspoken language.

Josephine was born to bear the heavier of the two crowns.

She was not a queen.

She was not his queen.

She was a King. An Outlaw King.

And like most royals of the New Kingdom, Josephine was born without a clue of the bluest river rushing through her. In fact, she expected nothing from her birth.

She was just happy to be here and hoped to fly under the radar long enough to eat all she could off this table of life.

You see, Josephine preferred to be invisible.

Her rightful throne remained empty while her regal ghost sort of moved about, letting her think she was an unwitnessed thing.

Josephine floated like a see-through kind of nothing while everybody else was so solid and so something. It was such a strange kind of freedom. It just didn't matter if she did or didn't, should or shouldn't. She just kept passing through all of the exhales and slipping silently inside the hot swoons, never knowing the parting of the crowd was for her.

The crown grew cold waiting for her silky skull to fill it.
This cellophane strolling of Josephine's made our King some kind of humble. The transparent crinkle made her buzz with a generous glow but she never felt it herself. She had no idea it would expose her to a dangerous future.

One night she stumbled upon the thrashing caverns built by the quick and the smart, the flawed and the flailing punk rock packs. Below the sidewalks of her working-class neighborhood, thumping through the garages of the thrift-store-clad daddies and dolls, she found a melodic noise she could sink into. She found a noisy kind of peace, a unique brand of deep suburban joy.

But this underground belonged to one and only one. Down there, The Monster was the God Almighty of Night. Suddenly, Josephine became solid and quite visible.

She flash-bulbed the playground where The Monster lived and ruled. He saw her loud and clear through the lightning of it. She pop-popped, her silhouette filling in and burning the picture of "Savior" into The Monster's psyche. Our Josephine never failed to trip the old wax wicks, never failed to tick, tick, boom, boom the room, but on this night she caught the eye of the hungry and, my darlings, on this night, the 20/20'd Monster was starving.

He wanted her to stay just like the image he'd captured. A hot and bursting icon, popping and sizzling at the other end of any room they occupied. Arms outstretched, in a pose of sacrifice to the Lord of the Underground.

He never really wanted to know Josephine. He wanted her to light his way, sitting rightly and bright beside him. She'd be his everlasting spotlight shining on his every move. He'd be witnessed always under the white-hot glory bulb called Josephine.

He'd make sure she'd never unplug from him.

He'd twist her in so hard, so tight, he'd make it impossible for anyone or anything to crack the vise of his grip.

Something in him knew she didn't belong under him or under anyone for that matter.

He knew it like he knew heavy, hard and hopeless.

He'd shove that knowledge down with all the other bad stuff and let the charm spill out and over his lips. Josephine's heart was wide open and her ears had never held such cream. She came to him easily and willingly and this only made him mistrust her more.

He schooled Josephine with his bullying lessons. Empty as he was, he made sure she stayed that way as well. He never filled her with anything solid, anything sweet. She ached with all that hunger a woman owns.

Only a man could feed her what she needed.

Only a boy would let her starve.

Josephine finally started to catch on.

The Monster knew it. He became very uneasy with the knowledge and he'd have to do something fast or she'd cave in and close up to him forever.

And so he gave her a glorious son, or maybe it was she who stole the babe from his loins. He never knew for positive if the little one was his gift or her burglary and at the time, it just didn't matter. The child was just the filler he needed to keep Josephine's withdrawal at bay.

Finally he'd come up with something to occupy the energetic girl and keep her out of his business of becoming larger than life, and for a while it worked. But eventually the distracting spell lifted and Josephine's hope for a real-life family smashed under the Doc Marten-clad foot-stompers of his precious Underground.

Little by little, Josephine and Sun-Son became their own kind of family, their heads pressed together in wonder as her boy's world began to yawn wide open. They thrilled in the simple and shared the impossible wish of true flight. They'd giggle as they'd each narrate their own version of what could happen if they could jump up and soar. Oh, the antics they'd pursue, with the security of knowing they had a ready and winged escape. In The Monster's presence, they'd speak their loving language with a shifty twist and a smile. Their unspoken understanding was unnerving to The Monster and was becoming more than he could stand. He began to panic, as if he were drowning in the wake of their path out of there. He loved the boy, in his own way he truly did, but The Monster had to come first. He now feared he wasn't even a number on her list.

He almost ran out of ideas when Josephine finally took the boy and ran out on him.

Almost.

He still had one.

Josephine made the necessary half-and-half arrangements, and he made the necessary miserable, brutal and frightening.

He'd end this thing, this Josephine.

He planned it down to the number of steps he would take toward her and the number of strides he'd need to get away from what was left of her.

Her hope for a grown-up kind of split was high and she trusted him against everything that rang and banged red against the setup. Her newfound hope must've silenced the alarm.

He found a gun and placed it heavy in his shaking hand. He bounced it on his palm. He smiled. It was his weekend so he stowed the boy with his mother. She'd be good for something, for once.

He set it up with a sweet-voiced call from a borrowed phone.
Josephine was already on her way to what she thought was an almost-perfect life. She'd found a man, the kind and knowing Saint, a quiet and stunning man who understood and loved her as a

woman should be loved. So much so that she was already swollen with his child. She was drunk with all of it.

She didn't want to suspect on that dusky night. She didn't want to add another bad road to the map of their relationship.

But they wanted two different things.

Josephine wanted life.

The Monster wanted her dead.

It was almost too easy, and the sight of Josephine bounding up round and baby-filled struck him sideways. It was a sucker punch as far as he was concerned.

He filled with a hate he never imagined existed.

Josephine was truly gone from him.

She stretched out her arms and welcomed this new beginning to their end, and he pulled out the pistol and blasted.

He fled faster than he ever had and left her there for the usual scavengers.

He tried to shake her last expression from his memory.

She didn't look scared or angry. She looked surprised. Could she have really expected him to take this? Did she really think he'd let her get away with getting away?

Josephine was a fool.

The crime created him. She was the master of this invention.
He was a new thing now, sewn together with angry fibers and filled with boiling black blood.

The blame didn't take care of the guilt. It didn't. It became thicker and grayer with every passing second.

He felt the hang of the curse, lowering, weighing him down.
He waved it away and took to lying soft between the finest of thighs. Only the image of his maker could prop him upright.

He fell furious toward the imposters, cursing the life and the death of Josephine.

He finally confessed this fact to himself out loud, as if to rid his cock of the so-called curse. The confession just didn't do its job. It wasn't just the look or the feel of her but the essence of Josephine that haunted him. It was the power. She charged him with an energy he'd never been able to afford. He owed her a value coins and paper didn't carry. The Monster never even attempted a remittance. It was he who was the fool.

The losing of one's king leaves a subject with nobody and nothing to serve. It made The Monster even angrier than he ever expected to be. Emptier. It made him lash out at the very thing he worshipped. Kill it down and it will be gone, he figured, no more ghostly wisps from that being.

He'd thought he'd planned it pretty well. Getting a pistol was easy as long as you assure them you won't kill a god. As long as you assure them that the toothpick you're chewing on isn't the femur of some poor, unsuspecting Jesus.

He was as good as a game show host, convincing them to look the other way towards maybe even a better prize. He stole a moment and left a receipt of grief on the world. This ripple would indeed change the future of innocents as every king's slaying has done before.

What about the baby?

That being inside Josephine wasn't a finished prince. He'd have to end the babe as well.

It would kill the Saint. The thief deserved it. He had taken away his Josephine, and now The Monster would end the child.

There. Done and done.
Silence.

That was all he heard.

It rang so loud it broke a barrier in his heart.

He'd expected the world to roar, but nothing and nobody really screamed for Josephine like he thought they would.

Blood is stickier and thicker than he thought it would be, too.

The feel of it stained him more than the color. The red of her personal mess would soon fade, he was sure of that. Soon, he could get back to the business of being. It was just a matter of time.

It was better this way, he thought. Better for him, of course, and that's all that ever mattered.

He rode away that night waiting for the lightness. Surely when the curse lifted he'd feel it, right? His head would rise, his cock would too and there would be no more lifeless bit for him to trouble over.

No more half-hearted parting of the milky white seas.

He still couldn't shake the other guilt. It felt like he was cheating. It felt wrong and not in the good way, brother.

Inside anyone but her and he felt like a liar. The great explosion had gone from an atom bomb to a firecracker.

He needed the light and heavy of his creator to really boom.

You know a man can conjure up just enough to get there, but wilting is a possibility now and it never was with her.

Did she realize the hold her gaze snapped? He was forever captured in the all seeing lens of Josephine and the new image was not as wonderful as it once was.

She moved inside of him as he did in her. It's sort of a premeditated revenge. Yeah, he thought, that's what it is. Like she knew how to haunt him all along.

He wasn't cheating. He kept telling himself that as he deflated out of another one.

He looked down on her and slid off. He looked down on her even from his side of her bed.

She looked up at him wondering if it was her doing.

Wonder till your scalp bleeds, honey; it ain't gonna get done tonight.

He'd just go home and get Josephine out of him. He'd come back when he was clean again, when his blood spanked his veins like he owned them.

Josephine left shorelines of scars.

Yeah, this one will do until time shot Josephine out.

Lately, The Monster had started looking behind him for no apparent reason. A pulse of sorts, a steady stream of kicks had been double beating behind him. It thumped softly at first then slowly, surely, it began to get quite thunderous. Especially at night. He tried to stay ahead of it, duck and outrun it, but he couldn't shake the throb of something following his guilty footsteps.

Stroke fast, he huffed, and drive even faster.

Chapter 8

The Saint is Broken

His love for her was ancient. When she touched him, it seeped into the cracks he didn't even know he needed filled. Some kind of cement, that woman made.

His woman.

Josephine.

The Saint shoved his head in his hands and felt the full weight of the sobbing stones. He missed her. He missed her son and he missed his baby. He was that empty kind of heavy. The Saint fell open.

She had mixed bad dust and rotten blood to make that Monster. It was hard to believe his very own Josephine had practiced the sin of creation.

What faulty powders she did grind? What dirty blood had she infused? A cowardly mix, it was. She couldn't help it. Josephine always saw something in nothing. She poured life into the hollow without so much as a drip or drain. She filled and filled. She left nothing empty.

But that creature of hers, that Monster, he came out porous. Every bubble burst and dried quickly to create yet another serious hole. Why didn't she abandon the shape and the form? The Monster sopped her up like a cement sponge, ever dry and always thirsty.

Couldn't she feel the sapping, the dangerous sucking of that thing? Didn't she care anything about her own time here? Didn't she know she'd be so needed and wanted, didn't she trust in that?

The Saint was past madness. He'd sunk beneath the grieving and invented a new kind of seething. He turned inside out.

Well it didn't matter now, didn't matter what clock, calendar or newfangled timepiece Josephine used to measure the value of her existence. The Monster had indeed disassembled her, springs and all. The Saint tasted the fury of it, like rot in his mouth.

That giant had stopped his child from ever ticking. That crust took his woman away. The Saint bowed deep and folded in half. His ache separated his muscle from his bone and he sobbed from the marrow melting into pure, liquid agony.

That vile, pulsing thing still walked in a coward's shadow while Josephine's veins poured out onto blessed hot sand, into the ruddy mud leaving her the stillest still, a sudden portrait he couldn't rip or erase.

Life will always be wrong here now. He hurt so hard he could feel his cells screaming inside his tubes.

He'd end that Monster and then end his own pain as well.

Where would he find that balloon of faulty meat and irreverent bone? And how would he pierce it dead, dead enough for all of them?

That's a task in need of a lot of blade. He'd forge it himself if he had to.

A new train of thought had left his rational station.

This was the only beginning he had left, the relief of a well-planned end.

Chapter 9

Josephine Reunites with Baby Dagger

Josephine knew that girl. The one in the booth on the left. The one she was going to deliberately sit behind, she and the boys.

The girl was with somebody, nobody Josephine recognized but oh man, he was familiar.

He was slicked back and greasy, bedeviled and dirty with a low-slung brow. He was the kind of cheap hoolie that made Josephine snarl that sideways smirk, a tell she kept to herself tonight. Her lashes lowered as she ushered her princes forward.

She and the boys slid inside the tuck-and-rolled vinyl booth unnoticed. The short and silkies on Josephine's neck stuck straight out when she felt the girl's voice skitter up her nape.

Her name was Baby Dagger. They used to battle side by side in the days of the untried and true, exorcizing their wildest and wicked ways. A loyal soldier to Josephine's General, she was.

She looked thinner and her hair wasn't yellow anymore, but the woman was most definitely Josephine's Miss Bee Dee.

She'd taken her short and spiky bleach job to a level-one blue-black and added a foot in length. It worked very well on the weary warrior. That big and bobbing top-shelf bounce was still working too.

But Baby Dagger wore an expression Josephine had never seen smeared across her smooth, flat face. Defeat. She'd been broken with an unfair lash like a lame pony and Josephine felt her white skin heat with a protective mama-flush. It was strong and it was potent.

Her trance was broken by the chitter-chatter of Sun Son ordering the usual. She glanced under the blanket of the baby and felt the cool sweetness of a Moonface sigh. Sleep, sugar, sleep.

It always amused Josephine as she watched Sun Son's fingers fall like new on to the same old thing he always ordered: a grilled cheese sandwich, French fries and chocolate milk.

It made mama's mouth tip up at the corners. Even on a hard night like tonight, the Golden Ones could make her smile.

She ordered the steak, medium, and fries, for herself. She thought she might need the knife by the end of the meal, you know, for the rare and the cooked.

The rumble of Baby Dagger's monster made her swing hard and high from that same hypocritical star she gazed upon with her own creature.

Josephine was now deeply disturbed, and her sin of impatience was speeding toward her crimson fingertips with the velocity of a misplaced meteor.

The Waste that Miss Bee Dee was seated with rumbled low, and it made her old friend shudder. Josephine could feel it all the way through the padding and vinyl. He was opening Bee Dee's store with punches and lies and setting her price in his ever-ringing register.

Josephine made a new and good decision.

She jerked during their entire exchange while measuring the weight of the time and the circumstance. She counted quickly.

Luckily, this one came up under the fifteen minutes she needed to spend.

Josephine could smell the skunky scent of fear from her former soldier.

It made her temper rise, and she had to deflate the beast before it blew. She needed her senses, and she needed them ice-water still, flat and clear.

She suddenly remembered the warrior chant she and Baby Dagger used to call out from the bottom of every hole they fell into:

"Brandy slow
And whiskey quick
Dig my walls
You
Armed with a toothpick."

She felt the bellow puff up her sails, and she smiled again at the masterpiece of crayon and menu Sun Son was creating.

Josephine was tracing the parallel lines between herself and Baby Dee. They were so shamefully straight and similar, stubborn lines drawn by arrogant women.

Who were they to think they could fix somebody, anybody? They were wrong, that's who they were.

Baby Dagger's eyes finally met her former General's, and Josephine lifted her head nice and slow. The nod fell up two stories and defied the low. The King bid a high welcome for the both of them.

The Dirty Waste caught the glimpse and decided it was harmless. He lowered his growl accordingly, but Josephine's hearing was always cued into that hideous frequency. He could mouth his speech, and it would still scream inside Josephine's sensitive shells.

Baby Dagger was pleading. Her look was utterly helpless. She was just too tired to fight anymore.

The Waste started toward the men's room. Josephine sniffed. That's not the room for you, boy.

He owned nothing close to resembling a man. He was a fool and a successful one at that. He'd tricked himself into thinking he really was something more than a waste of blood, pumping through rubber skin, nourishing nothing. The red ooze just bounced around inside of him, in and outing everything that was pretending to beat.

Josephine informed Sun Son she was going to the restroom and to watch the baby like the pro he'd become. He nodded and smiled through the waxy colors and crumbs, patting the baby carrier gently. He was growing to be such a big boy.

She lifted her hips off of the hot red plastic and slid the steak knife down the front of her 524s like wiping icing from a cupcake. The blade lay against the thick of her flesh and it felt rather fine. She shot a look at Baby Dagger that coaxed a soft smile only a mother knew how to keep warm even during the coldest of intentions.

The look ordered her to watch the boys. It glared that she'd be back.

Baby Dagger acknowledged the look the way she did in the old days, with a slight bow of her head.

Josephine waited outside the bathroom door.

The Waste pushed it out hard, and Josephine stifled the slam with her hand.

He held in his startle at the sight of her, a coward's party trick.

Fool. You can't hide a jump from a King.

He'd mistaken her glance earlier as a "look", and this would be his final beginner's mistake.

He smelled like Tres Flores pomade and old beer. He wasn't very tall, but he stood over all sixty-two inches of Josephine.

He brought his stink in close, too close. She easily kept her steady.

"What might you want, hmmm?"

Did he actually think that fake drawl made him seem relaxed? That it made him sexy in a slow, southern way?

Of course he did. He believed all sorts of stories. He loved his tales so much he probably wrote them down on dollar bills that he spent only on himself.

"Whatcha got." Not a question. The notes lay flat until the last word and then they dropped two more. She was already two clicks past impatient for his wheeze and whimper.

He grabbed her by the hair and pulled her back into the bathroom. Nobody saw or cared.

Josephine let him push her rack against the linoleum tile glued on the wall, and she even let him twist her arm into the pose.

If this were her first introduction to this kind of dance, the steps would seem scary and maybe too weighty to overcome. The curtsy and the twirl would have been too much of a dizzy to unkink.

But this wasn't Josephine's first ball, and he wasn't her cruelest partner.

Her other arm was still free, and he was almost disappointed that the struggle in her didn't make a tangle; but it didn't deter him.

Make no mistake, Josephine was scared. Without that fear, she couldn't be brave enough to attempt what she was born to do.

He had his cock out quickly, and she felt him jerking it alive.

She grabbed it with her free hand, and he released her twisted right with a guttural groan.

He felt he was getting what was coming to him.

She knew he was.

These creatures are so one-celled.

With her right free she reached down her jeans and pretended to help him find his way in. She slid the skin-heated blade, serrated and dull, up, out and down on all his selfish wanting.

Off it went but not without some sawing and a tug or two.

His eyes bulged and he slobbered a bit. He fell to his knees. That's how he should've greeted The King in the first place. He drew his deepest breath to scream a note so high it reached only one finely tuned ear.

Josephine's.

She lowered her chin, knife in one hand, worthless, empty casing in the other, arms outstretched like his new savior.

Her eyes stared into his as they glazed.

She nodded and gave him a scolding look only a mother could give and said softly,

"Enough."

She tossed the member down the john and flushed. He turned a grayish white that meant he'd be passing out soon.

As he lay unconscious Josephine fashioned a tourniquet from a piece of his stained up t-shirt. It stopped the squirting just fine.

He'd live to wish he were dead.

Four and a half minutes in and she was done.

She washed off what little bit of his filth had splattered and went back to the table where her sons were guarded and fine, just as she knew they would be with her recovered soldier beside them.

Baby Dagger's eyes were wide and wishing as Josephine nodded and smiled again. She held out her freshly soaped hand and welcomed Baby Dagger back into her life.

She introduced the once and soon-to-be beauty to her boys and paid the check.

Josephine would do what she was born to do.

She'd sacrifice for the greater good.

She was no saint, no sinner, and in this new world, it didn't matter anyway.

The four of them tucked deep into the Lincoln and drove to their new home, wherever that was going to be.

Chapter 10

The Desert Royals in Exile

The four of them drove out into the fuzzy, husky morning haze. Baby Dagger sat at the right hand of her majesty, a soldier repossessed.

The golden princes were strapped tight to the leather bench in back. Josephine adjusted the rearview so she could see their mirror portrait the entire ride. She smiled the softest Mama smile.

Josephine's mind did a bend-back just for a moment. These boys, her lovely blue-eyed babies, they saved her. Before them she was invisible. Because of their existence, she now had a reflection of her own. When they were with her, she materialized wholly, completely. This singular thought gave The King much peace.

Josephine had wandered this earth see-through. It's the difference between low esteem and none at all. Having little, the soul feels everybody's watching, judging and having a not too kindly opinion of what they're witnessing.

No self-esteem, completely different. You feel nobody sees you at all. You wisp around, unnoticed. Doesn't matter if you're good or bad, ugly or pretty. It just doesn't make any difference. It's a warped kind of freedom.

For Josephine, it made every mirror a plain piece of silver glass, every picture a cardboard glossy bookmark. Whenever Josephine saw her face staring back from some shiny slab, she just didn't recognize that girl. She'd cock her head to the right and shrug.

Josephine tipped her lamps toward the corner of the Lincoln. She glimpsed her Baby Dagger. She looked peaceful, or what Josephine imagined the colors of calm to be. She buzzed with the rhythm of the ride and sighed sometimes with the rev.

She'd known Bee Dee since they ran dirty days and dirtier nights, back in the times when Josephine's cellophane fade came in handy. She'd cling to a wall or lean up a chair real nice, folding her arms against the ever-open upholstered ones. She'd give a nod to Miss Bee Dee and pass a key.

The shop girl would wink the john and shed a curtsy for Josephine before starting the date. She'd return with the gold and a glimmer of hope that maybe she'd pleased The Outlaw King. The opportunity to give Josephine pleasure or some glint of silver satisfaction confounded her majesty. Why they wanted to serve her never made sense back then.

Now she understood.

She and Bee Dee ran a few girls and made a few dollars and then a few dollars more. They knew how to make a quiet and keep it.

The hush made them a whip of gold, and it was easy for a time.

Then it got way too hard.

Too hard for Baby Dagger, anyway. She developed a shout that told way too much.

Bee Dee got caught up in a terrible mess.

She started chasing the girls they were selling, and then her sprint darted toward the dragon. She got in so deep with her jockey that he started to take the debt out of her very lovely flesh.

First it was just for him; then he passed the desperate soldier around.

Josephine lost her in the musty mitts of the Hollywood underground.

She never forgot The Jockey's crop and how he whipped her down and out in ten weeks flat.

He shot her with junk and filled her with garbage to keep her running in spinning circles right back to him for some more.

It was such a fast and dreadful track and such a defeating race.

Sometimes Josephine hoped she was dead, lying in peace across her finish line.

When she couldn't look for her anymore, she sought the pinpricked wicked rider.

Fortunately for him, Josephine found him one trot too late, his head bashed in past the cement of the sidewalk.

She never felt bad about the smirk she wore when she recognized his ring from the imprint it left in Bee Dee's bleeding cheekbone on more than a few occasions.

She never felt bad about kicking his corpse either.

No one waited for him.

All of the storied thoughts raced past the picture in the rearview mirror and Josephine wondered the order of things. Was she living in the creation or was she the creator?

She found a clean and safe hotel with a nice café next door. She parked and paid and cautiously walked them all to the room.

Baby Dee didn't speak of the wince when she changed Josephine's dressing for her nor did she question The King's future intentions. She dared not trouble the water and she knew Josephine would flow slow and steady when they found a coffee and a safe and private sitting place.

Baby Dagger helped her tape and clean the wound up proper and waited for the slip of sleep to take them all before she allowed it to lean on her own lids.

Tomorrow, the new rules would be carved deep into the sandstone walls of the new frontier by the blade of its true and rightful King.

Tomorrow would be the beginning of Josephine's reign.

Chapter 11

Josephine and the Gentleman's Timekeeper

Deeper into that desert she had to go. Josephine knew this the way she knew anything. The ticking. That constant tock knocking inside her bone-ball reminding her that life indeed had its own schedule and was hell bent on keeping it.

She scooped up her clan and loaded them into the black dragon.

How had everything come to this?

She let the question mark slide off and stick itself to the hot morning pavement and drove over it nice and heavy, never looking back.

The vibration of the great roaming beast lulled her into some kind of old sweetness. She tried her hardest to whip it off and make room for maps and plans of attack, poses of defense.

The smell of the leather and thick oil was too much for her senses today. This was the perfume of their past, Josephine and The Saint's.

She drew it in deep and held it like an opiate-dreamy drag. It buzzed a line through her and the course of action she'd take to get back to him.

Rolling inside his Lincoln sometimes soothed her a little, sometimes killed her even more. Today's sly blade was definitely the double-edged sort.

Josephine's head wrapped around one moment, one perfect recall as the road hummed beneath her.

His watch.

The Saint had always worn a watch.

It wasn't one of those pieces a boy hangs onto well after graduation.

It was a man's watch, one he obviously picked and purchased on his own; one he thought about and maybe saved for.

It was a gentleman's timekeeper.

Brushed dense silver and heavy with a slight dip of a hang about his strong wrist, a simple and elegant face. She saw how it separated his hand from the rest of his arm and how its charming gleam made her look up from that point, all the way up his pressed white sleeve, rolled just below the elbow. She blushed when he caught her.

She felt obscene.

She felt handled.

She felt like a woman.

He smiled reassuringly, and she had to look away.

Josephine, from then on, felt like a lady in his presence.

In that seemingly benign instant, he made her better and closer to the person she was supposed to be. People can do that sometimes.

She wasn't brought into this world to be filled with womanly intentions, nor was she molded with the soft hands of a feminine artist.

Josephine's wolves, finished early with the business of raising her, released the last of their litter into the wild way too soon. They were not as insecure about her survival like they were with her brother and sister.

Her mother and father had used most of their parental energy on the first two and trusted Josephine to finish the job of growing up on her own. A strange confidence it was and a very twitchy gamble.

Josephine's appearance intruded on the content family of four, a clan without the need of another soul.

Her siblings already steady in their roles and rituals, happy in their social circles and station, had no need or desire for another child in the family.

Her sister made that fact ice clear.

She was quite content being the only girl and the youngest. She was her Daddy's Princess, and she wasn't going to give that up. Ever. She'd ignore Josephine's existence successfully until she married and moved out.

Josephine understood her sister's denial. It made perfect sense to the misplaced King. Her sibling was only fighting for what she felt was rightfully hers, and you just can't argue with the deserving.

Her brother was well into his own life by the time Josephine could wobble over to him. He actually liked his youngest sister but the early steps of this quick baby confounded him. She seemed complete at birth and didn't have the need for a patron saint of any kind.

The strikingly handsome boy wore the confidence of being their mother's favorite and had the rest of the family's admiration without question. It set him up and put him over to a higher place, his pedestal always infinite and climbing.

They did share some good things, quiet and thoughtful the both of them, but the same same's ended there. He'd never make a grown-up connection with the strange little girl.

Josephine knew her extra beat disturbed the rhythm of this family. She tried to pound in time but her syncopated click only caused skips and missteps in their greater song.

Cacophony.

Josephine, more than anything, wanted to become somebody they'd just want around, a complimentary melody or phrase, a sweet note in their incredible symphony.

She just kept tripping the tune.

Josephine found shadows and distances to house her, ones that were close enough for her to make it home on time for dinner, the only bell she was required to answer.

Deep inside the suburban skeletons of almost-finished tract homes, Josephine would wish hard on a five-pointed star.

While she was looking skyward through the plywood and webs of freshly cut wires, the four sides of her family closed into a box and shut tight.

Star shine wasn't anything they really wanted or needed to see.

She faded away, and her brightness dulled from their vision, and they went on with their day-to-days missing nothing.

Josephine missed everything.
She became bone achingly lonely.

She kept to breathing by staying away from the eaters of the young and tender. She held onto what little she had and kept journey-light for a very long time.

She traveled everywhere looking for somebody who might be waiting for her.

She found so many waiting for anybody. They would rattle together for a while and when the shaking stopped, she'd pull away and reopen her veins, floating away on the thick red hope of branded arms, etched with the nine lovely letters belonging to a clueless royal.

Josephine's journey forged armor.

She came back to her land a stranger, unrecognizable and unheralded. She made no claims and made no sound as she settled softly into the working-class valley she was born into.

Josephine had always enjoyed the luck of just being here, safe and healthy, and thanked a big unknown something every day for it.

She had made up her own religion and carried around her own set of stone-carved commandments. She even found some new sins to be forgiven for and scratched them upon the bottom of those heavy tablets.

She became a woman without knowing what one was and lived by her odd-shaped rules faithfully.

Josephine never took it for granted. To just wake and walk and wonder, it was a child's jig she danced in between the hard and grown-up march of responsibility.

Life was twirling her to the point of dizzy until the day The Saint gallantly cut in. He was one smooth waltz, he was.

That first night she met him, she had to blink over and over, squeezing the vision of this man into the present. He looked like

Hollywood's pictured past. His thick, dark hair parted on the left and slicked perfectly away from those deep-set dark eyes. The dimpled chin and wax-perfect skin wore such a calm and honest expression.

He was everything she never knew she wanted.

Josephine's eyes cleared when she heard Sun Son laughing in the back seat. The reverie ripped off and left a hole in the new scenery ahead.

Josephine had landed.

She planted Baby Dagger and the babies in a sweet little hotel up the road from the ugly nest she was to occupy this evening.

There was a good and tacky red den up the way where she'd try yet another quick occupation. New at something again, she was never comfortable with that. For the babies, she rationalized and reasoned. It crashed against the stones of "no" she'd kept in her head since forever but the banging would be a necessary distraction if she was really going to go through with this.

Josephine bathed the boys, put them to bed and sang them to sleep with a vacation song in C major. Baby Dagger was such a deep soldier, Josephine nodded her in on the way out and Bee Dee planted herself firmly beside them.

Down the road to the angry room Josephine went, to a place conveniently located next to a crashing boom room just like the ones she used to boss around her own Betties.

Now it was her turn. Now she was both employer and employee.

She spotted as she was eyed. All reasons for occupation were clear here.

How did everything come to this?

Chapter 12

Josephine Finds Work

He walked straight forward with a crooked purpose, pushing through the hidden door, opening wide the end of the line for Josephine. He was a practiced buyer here. His gaze circled the red cave, soaring up and down, his cashy jet landing smack dab on our snow-white King.

The banging stones in Josephine's head grew louder the closer he came.

Oh, those dependable and defiant rocks that had always tumbled with the loudest clack of "no" and "never".

Tonight they were betrayed, robbed of their purpose.

Josephine let the wave of thumping music drown them out.

She leaned back and waited for his approach.

This was one of a zillion holes where the mangy manes gathered, sporting their phony crowns and strutting like vacationing majesties, unashamed of the banded finger full of golden glint shooting rays all about the room.

Faulty lions the lot of them, sauntering over painted concrete floors and pointing dull-clawed filthy sausages at their quests for the evening.

Josephine had once guided these unruly rulers toward her very own sweet and fleshy herd.

Now she was the lone animal.

He plowed through the crowd and stopped in front of her. He parted his thick drape of a mustache and sneered through chiclet-capped teeth spurting from his fat cheek.

Thick with entitlement he was, squeezed into expensive clothes and shoes bought by a lucky life. His was a most certainly undeserved wealth. He was the poorest kind of rich.

A Fatted Duke.

Josephine sniffed no kindness from him, just the cheap scent of Buy-A-Betty cologne. It was embarrassingly familiar.

She met him easy. She played him easy. He submitted in the simplest way. She threw out the numbers that dripped off the crystal clock in the corner. They matched the number on the key. See? Easy.

Josephine started to feel angry and she grew even madder as they stepped closer toward the marked door she'd rented for this occasion. She was hot and not herself. She wasn't anybody. She couldn't be anybody tonight while being a mother.

She had to pull this off.

How?

The question set off an avalanche.

The boulders tumbled and slammed hearty dents inside her globe. Josephine's shape did change.

She'd have to forget about everything and everyone for an awfully long and overticking hour.

It would prove to be one of Josephine's most memorable sixty.

She walked ahead of him, and he smacked her heart shaped ass through the rented arch, swinging his hard, hairy arm like an apey croquet mallet.

That stinging swat ignited something unexpected. The pain made its way past her repulsion and pride.

It stuck onto an untouched piece of her porcelain.

That ass-smack conjured a vision of sizzling wives much too powerful and pretty, bullied into a numbed and bored existence.

She could see them tapping their unscuffed pointies, watching the Big Bens and silently scolding their fatted cowards as they staggered through early-morning doorways.

The sting of his fleshy, fingered paddle lingered, and it splashed everything over the edge she'd been holding together all evening.

He grabbed at her and tried a kiss.

His clipped mustache was boar-bristle hard, and it punctured her cushion lips with painful piggy pricks.

He squeezed and pulled and pushed and tried to get past the pale steel.

Her head was a banging ball.

Josephine lost her temper.

Something lit up and started to burn in her cavities. A new flame of logic was fanned and flared. Possibilities and hope licked up her spine and she became an uncontainable blaze.

Josephine's wheels peeled out in reverse. This was not what The Duke had paid for. Lucky for her, he was feeling adventurous this evening and hell, this might even be fun if she can keep it up lap after lap without flattening his puffiness.

He lurched forward and pulled his smooth manicured hand back, slapping her fine-boned cheek.

This was better than he thought.

Better than he bought.

Josephine let her head snap to the side, and she turned it back toward him without expression.

She'd been on both ends of this kind of slap before. It wasn't new.

And its ringing wasn't as loud as the rocking of her stones.

Their tumbling turned into a chant.

Nobody waits for him.

Nobody.

The vintage pitcher on the chipped-up dresser looked close and it looked heavy, hearty and inviting. It almost smiled with a shiny answer to this spreading, swelling problem.

He was sweating slime now, hard and showing. He tugged his pants away, then his briefs.

The Fatted Duke shoved these all down and offed the shoes and socks, kicking them into the rest of the pile. He unbuttoned the shirt as if to bare a real man's chest, only to reveal a simple baboon.

She couldn't help but stare. There it was, his reason for living, leaving, loving and lying.

He looked quite proud.

He felt a new and giant power with this Betty, and his little godmade shaft made like a tightly twisted balloon.

Josephine was a gate crusher when it came to dam builders like him. She'd destroy what she never meant to erect.

On this night she saw the purpose of her being as clear as her backward image in the giant mirror facing the purple velvet rumpled bed.

On this night, she found her crown and placed it squarely on her royal pate.

He clawed at her shirted shoulder.

The pitcher splintered against a sharper-toothed chair. The finest shard jutted out like a dagger from the handle still in her hand.

It was smooth in its entry.

It was just as smooth in its reentry.

He greased over, staying hard as he crumpled at her feet.

He stared up at her disbelieving this to be his end.

The spike of an authentic sword can indeed be surprising.

She whispered things to this leaving being, brows arching over the center of her royal nose.

Little murmurs and mumblings, a language only a true King could utter.

"You're killing me," he sputtered, as if the very act could be reversed now.

She nodded her "yes" like an aristocrat.

He passed, and Josephine showered in the room he paid for.

She gathered herself and his wallet and strode out as if she was covered in robes of soft-spun gold and dipped in powdered marble.

Finally the stones had stopped slamming, not even a tap.

The primate had had a pocketful of charging and she knew how to juice the skins anonymously dry.

It was quite enough to get what she needed, and he'd not be missed.

Nobody waits for him.

She'd find a nest and make it kind enough for a working girl and stern enough to ward off the nonsense. She had great rhythm for that. She knew what, who and how to sell and didn't judge, buyer or seller be.

The drive was fresh, and it was still quite early. She couldn't wait to get back to the sweet room with her sugar boys and crystalline soldier. Tomorrow she'd take them to safer digs and plan the battles of the new war.

She knew just where to go.

The rattling of the rocks had been silenced.

All she could hear now were the soft notes of a vacation song in C major.

Chapter 13

The Madness of the King

Bullock stared at the report on his desk and it stared right back at him with haunting hazel eyes framed by the long dark hair of the petite stranger he was dead set on deciphering.

The detective had been waiting for something to split wide open and there, splayed before him was the gaping bloody clue that would lead him to the woman he now knew as Josephine.

The name she gave at the hospital was the kind of fake that let the weary nurse know not to waste any more breath digging any further, and ridiculous enough for Bullock to figure out she'd simply tweaked her first name into two: Josie Fine. It seemed more a wish than a declaration.

The pictures that were snapped at the scene were as sloppy as the crime itself, but even through the shredded mess Bullock could see a rage as clear and as whole as a crystal ball.

He looked deep, all the way down to the shiny bone poking through the filleted fatality. This was not Josephine's fiend, he was sure of that.

The stabs were meant as a final halt, not a ready revenge. It seemed the lovely lady had changed her mind, and the manicured sap had not.

That conclusion made Bullock smile, the wrongest right thing he could do at a time like this.

This one seemed to be a first, and the detective would've bet any amount of cash this fat cat wasn't her last.

Something had cracked and shifted inside Josephine, and a cold panting blustered out from the new flaw. Bullock shivered from the familiar draft.

If he could feel it, they could too.

He decided he had to get to her first.

Chapter 14

Josephine's Pennybrides

Josephine settled them all into a sun-dipped compound made up of three large trailers.

Two of the ready-mades were bridged together by a covered hallway. They would house the King's business of Betties.

The lefty was a bar with a blazing granite rock fireplace shooting all the way up the starry high ceiling. This bar had a thick and plushy sitting room that wrapped around the resin-dipped mahogany liquor leaner that separated the wanted from the waiting.

Toward the back of Lefty's Bar was where the tunneled hallway opened and emptied into the mighty righty where the Betties' bedrooms were. That's where they'd lay the bodies down and turn the violent gasps to gold. Both were deep and red and warm.

The third structure was a good stroll away from the other two. Elder oaks bowed over the front porch and allowed The King and her princes their privacy. It too had a floor-to-ceiling fireplace, one made of used brick which Josephine found quite charming. The inside was wombed with swirling and smooth wood walls.

The kitchen was surprisingly large and welcoming. A pink stove and fridge winked sweetly and the pristine white cupboards had lovely chrome handles that reminded Josephine of her grandmother's.

The bathroom had a clawed bathtub that thrilled Sun Son to no end. He said it was like taking a bath in the belly of an eagle.

There was a spacious back room for Baby Dee with a separate entrance and its own little sun porch that suited the soldier to a capital T.

Welcome to The Lost Chambers.

The sultry sand digs would serve them well for a while.

It was an odd stroke of luck and fate that Baby Dagger still had her feet dipped into the rubber lake of lovemakers. The procuring of the finest Betties was just a tattered black book away. She knew almost too many ladies and the auditions took two days too long, as far as Bee Dee was concerned. Josephine did indeed hold to a strict vision of loveliness and all new hires must possess the necessary evils.

First there was the sacred oct. They had to silhouette the number eight. The shape of the digit reminded Josephine of a racetrack and she liked them built for speed. All the ins and outs must curve toward the finish line every time.

Second on the list of demands was Josephine's need for contrasting, proper hues. If they came to The Chambers snowy fair, the hair must be black. Dark skin dawned platinum locks. Red hair was the wild card. Josephine would decide who'd go the way of the rosy.

The third requirement was the arrangement of things. Soft curls and waves brushed into framing old-odd perfection, bobby pins and rollers, scarves, merry widows, stockings and pumps. This is the uniform of the desired, according to Josephine.

The fourth rule was proper placement and content of personal art if there was any. Their skin could be sweetly stained with gardens of traditional flowers but she didn't care for the ink covering of their own buds. Breasts must be clear of markings. Lilies, orchids and roses might blossom under sparrows and dragons anywhere but on the belly, buttocks and breasts. The lick of the needle's tongue did indeed translate taboo into the language of dollars, but only if it was the frame, not the canvas. Josephine knew this for a fact

One by one, Josephine's modern day pinups came down off the garage walls of the Inland Empire, fingerprints, pinpricks and all, and put their dreamy extremes to work for The Outlaw King.

They'd now stand in animated third dimension, and they'd wall-to-wall the most exclusive brothel in the desert.

Josephine now housed a revved-up bevy of Betties like the low desert's never seen and never will again.

Here lie the Pennybrides.

Josephine was learning how to make money and make it fast. Know what you're selling and whom you're selling it to, set the price and never waver.

She saw to every financial arrangement through cameras and Baby Dagger. No wheeling dealing. A number chosen by Josephine was given to the girl and her suitor for the evening. This number was written on the finest of stationery etched with a broken red heart repeated endlessly around the edges. The number was cursived by The King herself and it was non-negotiable.

The beings she lured here, the kind that would take ever so generously to the Pennybrides, didn't like the force of money being the leg spreader, the mouth opener. Josephine understood that.

Josephine didn't like that kind of exchange either.

Each dessert sliced the finest piece of sinner-saint pie. She couldn't care less if you did or didn't, there wasn't a gavel or robe in Josephine's character. She reserved judgment for true crimes against the innocent. The grown-ups here were anything but.

Nor was she a Pennybride's friend. She was not their lost mama or their confidant.

She was their boss. THE boss.

Josephine would take care of them monetarily as long as they took care of her in exactly the same manner. She'd keep them as safe and warm as was heavenly possible and teach them to buy their freedom to use any way they pleased.

That was their true salary.

Josephine's teachings would show them how to be well and wonderful in this world.

And of course there were the rules, laws that were strictly enforced and not repeated.

Pennybrides would bang-bang while Josephine took responsibility for each and every shot, hit or miss.

The Brides were forbidden to fraternize with the Golden Princes. Only Baby Dagger earning her ten percent of the place could speak to and care for them and only what when and where Josephine allowed.

They boys were never to see, speak of or visit the Lefty or the Righty. Ever.

Josephine purposely rumored that disappearing was but a sweet slip away if a Pennybride was to make the mistake of disorder and the stories of previous rule-breakers murmured throughout The Lost Chambers until each and every ear was warmed with the warning.

So paint your toes and fingers the bloody red that's set out for you and get on your backs, my Betties, my sweet, sweet Pennybrides.

Soon, you won't need a King anymore and she won't need you. Your roads will split apart and run parallel, never crossing again. Accept her fill and you'll never ever be empty.

Good night, sweet kittens, good night.

Chapter 15

Josephine Can't Stand a Betty with a Question

It wasn't a silent coldness or some dopey damage that made Josephine the quiet type. It wasn't some delusion of importance or cause that kept her mouth shut.

It was just plain old-fashioned toe-tapping finger-pounding impatience.

The wasting of time was the number one sin scratched deep at the top of her heavy tablets.

Josephine didn't take to waiting in line, online, over the line, under the line or anywhere near the unrelenting straight and narrow. To hear something that meant nothing, to say something that meant even less was pure robbery. Life was just too tragically short.

Josephine's clock was ticked off and done, done, done.

The Pennybrides were another long-winded and wound-up story.

They lived for a good talk and loved a stolen listen even more. Their mouths and ears flapped wildly within the confines of The Chambers, causing tiny tornados all day long until the nighttime gave their mouths more profitable things to do.

When Josephine would swagger into Lefty's they'd hush so obviously. She purposely made her stomp louder than the twitters and giggles, and the Pennybrides would take the warning well, snapping to a mute salute.

Josephine would look past their curvy outlines as they chirped a reverent, “Hello, Ma’am,” waiting for her nod.

Josephine would fill her chest with the scent of fresh Betties and lift her right eyebrow while gathering her thoughts and giving the ladies the once-over. She strolled the line and leaned into their necks one by one. She glanced the backsides and silked an upper arm. She chilled each one and the fluttering of their hearts pushed up the goose bumps that could only be raised by the stroke of their King. She’d tilt her head to the right and speak softly into Baby Dagger’s ever-present ear. She’d whisper what was done well, and what needed some fixing.

Twisting on her left boot heel she’d leave her soldier to relay the necessary repairs and their schedules for the day.

On one particularly stiff and busy Monday, Cecilia Pennybride stopped Josephine on her way out. The audacity of the move caught Josephine off guard, and she drew in her deepest breath, the kind she used to calm herself and warn others. On that Monday, the steep inhale failed to do its job on both ends.

Cecilia began nervously spouting unnaturally blue greetings and queries that would never come to her bright but simple mind. Josephine began to tap her toe as the Betty rambled through the matte red. She assumed the Bride was merely trying to make points with the boss. A puffed and powdered nose up the behind was not the way to win favor with Josephine. Bee Dee obediently appeared at her side awaiting the inevitable order of the whip and paddle before the flooding mistake drowned the entire bar.

The Betty began with pleasantries, and when they weren’t reciprocated, she got right down to the business at hand.
“You know, Josephine, we’ve never really talked. I’d really like to get to know you, yeah? I mean, just have a good old-fashioned hen party, just you and me”.

Cecilia smiled.

Josephine did not.

Baby Dagger began a rehearsed warning but Josephine touched her soldier's wrist. She was curious to see where this was coming from and where it was going. Bee Dee retreated and the Betty went on.

"I mean, none of us knows anything about you, really. We know stories, rumors, whatever. See, I'm the kind of gal that believes in being straightforward, you know? I don't like to talk behind people's backs or anything. If you want to know something, I always say go to the source, right?"

Josephine knew that any sentence starting with, "I'm the kind of *anything*" could only be the opposite of whatever descriptors someone was fooling herself with.

Cecilia laughed and tittered, shifting her weight from her left pump to her right. She was almost shaking. Almost. She seemed most dutiful. She pressed further.

"Like, are you married, 'cause I thought you used to wear a ring or something, I, I thought I saw a ring, um, on your left, uh, hand." Cecilia twisted her white hair around her brown finger and Josephine began to focus on the gesture and not the words. She raised her arches and chin slightly, looking down the royal nose and staring directly into the Betty's dark eyes.

The absence of answers gonged a deafening ring of silence. Finally, the chatty Bride heard it.

The still-assembled Pennybrides were aghast and coming apart at the seams. They dared not look toward the mayhem. Instead they directed their curly-framed and shocked expressions inward. They couldn't imagine what Cecilia was thinking and they thanked their heavenly mothers and fathers for granting them enough smarts not to do such a stupid, stupid thing.

They also thanked the saints that gave them their razor-sharp hearing.

Cecilia persisted, now obviously carrying out some sort of mission, too far gone to feel the icy rush of cool from her King. She shifted to another subject, another kind of questioning that was probably written down somewhere.

But by whom and why? This interview was coached, coaxed and memorized, no doubt about it.

The Pennybrides couldn't ever remember hearing of a Josephine that would let a verbal assault go on as long as this one. Was she so like a lion that she enjoyed playing with her prey before devouring it?

Cecilia was a runaway train now, railing too fast to brake.

"Um, yeah," she continued, "You know, I thought I heard you one night after a party playing a guitar or something. It was really cool, that you know how to do that, play and sing or whatever. That was you, right?"

She trailed off and her eyes darted everywhere but forward. Her hands twisted each other fervently and her toes pigeoned inward. She realized too late she had crossed a very deep line.

It wasn't so much the accosting that alarmed The King. It was the subject matter. She asked about a life long before this one, the one nobody here could possibly be privy to.

The hairs on Josephine's neck rose like a grove of red flags and she cocked her head again toward the side adorned with Baby Dee. Enough.

Josephine whispered to her soldier, all the while keeping her gaze locked onto Cecilia's, no expression, just a hypnotizing hold, a grip the Betty couldn't break.

That Bride got a good shiver and shake, she did, and the exchange between Josephine and Bee Dee seemed to go on forever. All she could do was wait.

Josephine knew right away it wasn't Cecilia's own fat reds that were doing the asking. Somebody else was using that mouth and whoever it was, she was going to find out.

She turned and walked away without a word to the Bride, let alone an answer to the borrowed questions.

Baby Dagger stayed behind and earned her pay.

The soldier reminded Cecilia that you never address Josephine directly unless the boss prompts you first to do so and you never question her about her life, ever. She said it with an upper arm squeeze that weakened the Betty's entire body.

Baby Dee went on to school Cecilia while sliding her hand up and guiding her through the tunnel by the back of her slender neck. She instructed the misguided Bride that if she ever again felt the need to speak to Josephine it would be in her best interest to pillow that pucker and walk as fast as she could in the opposite direction. With that last lesson, she pressed the soft and slender cocoa stem hard enough leave a little bruise of a reminder.

She opened the door to Cecilia's room and filled it with its occupant, throwing her hard over the threshold onto the bed. She instructed her to stay, just like the bad kitten she was, and stay is just what that Pennybride did.

Josephine was disturbed. She knew the questions came from a buyer. He'd filled that Betty's mouth with the failed interview using the poor woman as his shield. He had most definitely been inside that Pennybride's head and he filled an empty hole she had kept hidden from the world. The coward must've been quite purposeful in his pump.

Josephine's tock was ticking loudly.

She tapped her own blood-red smacker with her matching fingertip.

For your sake, little one, I hope somebody waits for you.

Chapter 16

Monday Night is Beauty Night

The Brides were all a-fluff and aflutter. They hadn't stopped talking about what might be their colleagues' first and last mistake. It gave them all a good rile.

Cecilia knew the rules as well as they did, and they couldn't imagine what kind of desperation drove her to such a futile and dangerous destination. They cut off all association with the tainted Betty. None of them wanted to get anywhere near that kind of fresh failure.

Josephine noticed the shunning and took it into account.

The Pennybrides were treated very well at The Lost Chambers, and because they were chosen to work their magic there, they almost felt like they'd won something. For once in their lives, some of the beautiful Betties felt a little lucky.

And Josephine kept them an impeccable lot, primped proper and perfumed, coiffed and coutured. She brought the doctor by regularly and kept them on the clean, inside and out. They felt a sense of pride, some of them for the first time in their hard-candy lives.

And Monday night was Beauty Night.

Flo and Toppy, Josephine's talented and trusted hairdressers, were the best of their kind, schooled and tooled in the refined art of the shampoo set and finger wave. They showed up promptly at six, white, crisp and upright, looking as pretty as the ones they served.

They dyed, clipped, curved and caressed the Betties with sweet smelling sprays keeping the softest curls in place.

Brown-blacks, blue-white platinums and rolling rusty reds were administered to the rooted locks. Luster had made a comeback at The Chambers.

The stylists spoke little except to each other as they synchronized the shampooing, the setting, the comb-out and the coif. Their no-nonsense approach was worth the double-time wage Josephine gladly paid the talented twosome.

Miss Winnie was the esthetician. She had taught The King herself the spells and secrets of tending to her own steely silk.

Miss Winnie saw to it the fascinating faces were creamed, vacuumed, peeled and scrubbed. They were softened, soaked, stained and flooded with rich-smelling liquids and tonics from all over the world. She showed them true beauty was an authentic smile and all the lines that came along with it. Keeping it all clean was key.

Originally from Belgium, the beautiful seventy-six-year-old had a fine and upstanding demeanor and a board-straight posture that commanded everybody's full attention and respect. Josephine would not tolerate back-talking or swearing around any of the technicians and if any Betty so much as chirped a cuss, she'd remove them from the festivities and send them to their rooms uncurled, unpolished and undone.

Even Josephine joined in on Beauty Night.

She rather liked all the push and pull, the rubbing up, down and sideways. She liked her hair tugged gently into a stunning coif of a more innocent time long past. She wanted to not only prize the ladies with what may be their only exhale of the week but to reward herself with a good long sigh as well.

Top to bottom, bottom to top, everybody looked like a pristine figure on the cover of a dime-store novel.

But on this particular Monday morning Cecilia had succeeded in tearing their coveted Beauty Night to shreds. She'd ripped a hole in their primp bubble universe and let in a dirty and viral unrest. It would take a whole lot of smoothing to slide forgiveness back down their slick valves.

Cecilia tasted the bitter of the regret and hung her head for all of them to see. She felt a new kind of defeat.

The Brides' dinners were served in their rooms that evening and they devoured juicy T-bones sauced aplenty with hot and bloody resentment. It didn't go down well.

Baby Dee instructed them to wait until Josephine came for them, and this made their simmer steam through the ceiling.

The King's heel-toe boot beat always sounded so pointy, such a hurting sound. It rattled the lovelies as it made its way down the hall toward their bedrooms. Each beauty sat upright on the edge of their bed and prayed for its passing.

Josephine opened each one of the doors, one after the other, as she passed. After the last she stood quietly at the end of the hallway. She instructed them to go to Lefty's and enjoy their Beauty Night as usual. Even Cecilia. Especially Cecilia.

You could almost taste the collective sigh as they padded through the tunnel toward their well-deserved appointments.

Josephine waited for the conversation to kick in and when the volume reached the perfect pitch, she slipped into Cecilia's quarters.

She didn't know what she was looking for, but she knew she'd find the answer somewhere between the crisp white softness and the hard black wood floor.

Josephine looked around and for the first time since opening up the gothic brothel, really took it in.

She decided that she rather liked the smell of the bounce in there, the sweet and dusty vanilla with a float of cherry-red air. The curves creased everything with such telling lines. This place had shaped into a stunning sculpture carved by women who make their living in the linen. Josephine didn't touch a thing for several minutes.

Cecilia's room was just as neat as it should be, but tonight Josephine wasn't looking for the required and the obedient tidy. No, tonight she was looking for the mess.

Josephine's hazels grazed the creamy walls and dark-walnut varnished floors. They landed on the Betty's well-used writing desk. Scribbles and scrawls littered the top of it like suicidal leaves. A calendar lay near an old blue pencil. The pages were dog-eared and marked throughout with X's and O's. Nothing unusual there.

Josephine brushed some of the squares aside and slid open the shallow drawer. There were stamps, old lipsticks and nail polish bottles. A little statue of the virgin rolled to the front. She was gray plastic with painted pink lips. Odd color for the Saviors Mother, she mused.

Josephine's eyes were drawn back to the date keeper. Cecilia had days circled and the words "reggies" and "newness" scrawled in her childish handwriting below most of the numbers. The descriptions were self-explanatory, no new tale told there.
As she closed the drawer she felt a sticking of sorts as it stopped midway. She opened and shut it, but it kept stopping in the middle.

Josephine felt the slide underneath for the obstruction and plucked out a pamphlet with a picture of Jesus or Shooter Jennings splayed and nailed to a cross. It had an inscription: To Cecilia. May you find your way through His way. J.
How sweet.

Cecilia had a converter.

A converter was a well-known stranger in the lovemaking business. They fell deep into the category of harmless fetishists and their get-off was based on the success of their impotent power of turning a bad girl good. As if there was such a thing as a bad girl.

Josephine shook her head. She was relieved.

She imagined him waving his boardwalk cross over Cecilia's forehead. She could see the Bride convulsing for him, somehow knowing this was what he was paying for. For the final hoot he'd plead salvation from a saint he didn't even believe in himself. He'd get hard witnessing the shaking she-devil, only to go home and spurt alone, swearing his was the only man-matter that could wash away all the sins of women. He'd feel ashamed and unwashed and he would shower for hours crying cowardly tears into the spray.

Josephine shook her head again and added an eye roll.

Converters almost never enter a Betty. They never allow themselves to feel the tender squeeze of the ample thighs, never get close enough to tip the wonderful hourglass of the truly ticking.

No, their bent was neither rare nor unusual. It's a known fact, some folks just like the company of a whore.

Josephine looked further down the hole and felt the stream of relief dam up.

The crimp in the hose was the scribble on the inside of the hidden booklet, a shorthand version of the failed interview, slapped on the page by a different hand, a heavy and slapping hand.

A man's hand.

And there was something else: a crooked and cursived "Josephine" written once and one too many times on the very last page underneath the picture of a Magdalene.

Josephine caved in.

The fear returned quickly with a broad slap.

This converter had come for her. He'd come from her past, a fervent and benign admirer maybe or a friend of a "friend." He didn't want a conversion. He wanted an exorcism. He wanted to flush Josephine out of The Chambers and back to her old and dangerous world.

Now it was her turn to shiver. She wasn't ready for any kind of reveal and she wasn't happy about the curtain being pulled back while she still held tight against the tugging.

He'd have to be excommunicated from this new church. Josephine traced the writing and whispered, "Who waits for you?"

She paced and sniffed and shoved the pamphlet back under the drawer, slamming it shut. She was vibrating. He was going to be shown a god or two but not the kind he prayed to.

Josephine's temper was lit.

She rummaged around a bit more and found the days he'd visited Cecilia. Four dates total and he had a circled number coming up. Tomorrow. He was a "reggie," a regular. Tuesdays were his plus days but he was going to be a minus in Josephine's book.

Josephine was holding toe on that cracked and broken Monday and she was already kicking it into the day that followed. Joseph. Tuesday. This was his day. Indeed.

Let him believe a fortune of favor awaits him in Cecilia's room.

Let him believe in the ever last, the never end, the sacred ride out of death's digs.

Josephine sighed the deep sigh. She had tried gods as a child. A catholic baby, Josephine had been baptized, communioned, confirmed and most certainly, eulogized since the Monster's gun.

She had tried so hard to feel that thing she saw in the believer's eyes, she just never got the gaze. Every incarnation of this bigger being that was formally and casually introduced only seemed more colorful. It never had the hazy see-through she'd been told it owned. To her it became more solid and bright like a character from some sort of pious comic or something. She began challenging the thing. Then she ignored it. Then she purchased objects that resembled the being whenever she ran across them in thrift stores.

Maybe that was the truest faith, the only believe-in she could come up with. To reject something you don't actually believe exists, well that's a kind of religion in a way. That's a kind of believing of sorts. Maybe she just felt that the rejection of your creator's creator was too much back turning for her and she just wanted open arms. Josephine was angry with herself for failing something she never had the chance to succeed in. She dripped some sad and left Cecilia's room just as she'd found it.

Josephine swaggered on back to the Brides and walked right through them. Miss Winnie looked up and saw the melancholy. She nodded a mama nod and Josephine wilted a little. She touched Bee Dee's elbow and led her back to the house. They bleeped up the client screen and brought up the dates for tomorrow evening.

There he was, sure enough.

Joseph, Tuesday at ten.

Chapter 17

The Church of Josephine

Tuesday had a sweetie-soft entry compared to Josephine's rock hard candy night. The dark seemed entirely too big and it hung heavy and mountain still, shadows on top of shadows. She checked the boys every three to five minutes and almost hoped they'd awaken. My goodness, those boys could sink a plush velvet when they wanted to. Josephine brushed the blond away from the tender, smooth foreheads of her princes and left them to their soft sighing and stirs.

The King tossed. She didn't care for confrontation, no indeed, and the anticipation of it made her wide-eyed and grumpy. She rubbed her head and stretched out ready. She felt robbed of an earned night's sleep by the time the orange ball rose, and she mumbled her complaints to nobody in particular as she brewed the morning coffee.

She stomped her way to Lefty's and readied the Brides for the evening's honeymoons. From her mouth to Baby Dee's ear and out again as usual.

Cecilia would be joining Sweet Georgia tonight. Josephine had arranged the party and a gentleman with a big heart and an even bigger balance would be patiently waiting for the pinup bookends at ten.

Cecilia reminded Baby Dagger of her Reggie around the same hour. "Not for you to worry about, doll," Bee Dee scolded. She motioned for her to get along and take her nonsense with her.

Baby Dagger was not amused by her earlier stunt and it showed. Cecilia was a bit relieved, actually. She had nothing for her client, not what he'd asked for anyway, and he seemed to bring the terrible troubles along with his armload of crosses and pamphlets.

The Bride didn't need any more tangles, and besides, that god he spoke of was the very same one that had sat on his righteous holy behind and watched while she was beat down by a very smelly and hungover stepmother. That same entity watched as she lay inside the broken skin, daring not a weep for that would bring on even more of a blood leaking. You can keep your blind and deaf god, she thought.

She grabbed another croissant and headed to her bath.

When the Inland Empire sun dropped deep behind the snaggle toothed San Bernardino range, Josephine matched the nighttime skin with her own version of the dark: black tee, black hair and black look. She kept it all in check so at any given moment she could really melt into what was to most likely be somebody's last starry sky. The blurriest of darks she was, too, making all her edges hazy and quiet. Not a stark horizon on her, just an almost-there quality that was more a shadow than a silhouette.

She sank into the big chair in Cecilia's room. All the rooms had one. The chairs resembled a martyr's throne, with a deep and low resting recline of sorts. Josephine had handpicked them herself, suited for any kind of reigning that might occur on these tiny kingdoms of sin.

She let the leftover hall light shoot a bit of its glow through the crack in the door. She sank in the chair so elegantly, one leg outstretched, one cocked up and ready in case a pounce was necessary. Her head was heavy to one side from bearing the imaginary crown dripping with its responsible stones.

Her reach was relaxed as her red manicure held the arms gently like tender claws.

Josephine waited.

The ladies' bouncing faded off into a predictable rhythm.

The slit of light stayed steady but it would soon blink with the passing of the visitor in the corridor. Josephine waited some more.

She heard a whisper. A call. It was his voice. It had a Southern California lilt to it, an accent that was born and raised here. The preach wanted to come out of that distorted mouth so bad, the kind of bellowing that blows the strands in your ears every which way but right. It makes your neck jerk and rip a bit. Josephine felt the irritation. It twitched inside her spine. She did not know this man but she knew his ilk. She was raised around hog-riding supposedly reformed addicts. They made Jesus their new pill and wanted you to swallow the sweet savior tab as well. They wanted you to down it with their swill of a sermon and nod off as if they'd just shot you up, shot you up good and tight.

Yeah, Josephine was familiar.

Only her head cocked, nothing else. She still held the arms of the soft throne, ten drips of red varnish visible even in the half-light. The light grew wider and then spread open just enough.

He whispered again for his Bride Cecilia. Josephine couldn't help the crooked grin. She squinted just a bit and let her lips relax before he could see it.

The light slashed across the calm recline of The King.

"Cecilia?" he asked.

No. Not even close.

He slipped past the still-too-stingy opening and gripped his readings to his chest closing the door behind him. He was tall, thin and dressed exactly as expected: plaid button down, blue department store slacks of some sort and the ever-present sensible brown shoes with quiet rubber soles. Behold the uniform of a humble man of god.

He clicked on the lamp and it splashed golden onto the entity that was Josephine.

He sucked in the illuminated air and took in the expanse of the vision of a small woman housing a gigantic fever. He sank slowly to his knees.

"Hello, Josephine. You came, I mean, you're here."

"Where else would I be, Joseph?"

The query was complete in its asking. He had no alphabet or syllables for a reply and that was the anticipated answer.

Josephine rose up and she rose well. Joseph remained committed to the kneel as he watched the rising of his Magdalene.

Her curves whipped up the sin in the room. The Converter had never suspected attraction. The bubble talk that surfaced in the baths of the Pennybrides never popped a word about her shooting slopes and valleys. The instigator of this job never mentioned it either. It took him by surprise.

Most of the chitter in The Chambers centered on that resilient silence she kept, the voice hardly ever heard that became so effective and memorable when it was employed.

The Brides confessed a fear and reverence toward Josephine that spun their yarns into tales of permanent take-outs and pouty mournings. She was a living fairytale of sorts.

His current employer had merely told him to be careful of the petite thing, that she was fast and she was quiet.

To Josephine, this intruder was lucid. She could see the veins and meat as they pumped and jerked, feeding his cowardly heart. She could tell he recognized her from words, not from any previous physical acquaintance. She knew most certainly he was sent.

Somehow they had a common body between them but she wasn't sure whom.

Josephine felt danger buzz inside her and the scary vibrate shook her to action.

"Get up," she exhaled.

He did.

Standing in front of her, she smelled motel soap. She didn't like the hard-cake perfume. Stale and flakey, it was. It tattled Joseph's temporary residence; the kind one uses to carry out orders.

He started to speech her. She didn't care for any kind of speeches. They all started and ended the same.

"Quiet down," she breathed, and raised her hand toward his vulnerable skull.

Josephine would bluff some kind of common acquaintance with the chance that Joseph would react. It was a healthy gamble.

"Where do you come from?" She wanted a name.

A lie tripped over his tongue. She asked something more specific.

"Who sent you?"

He was taken aback but not surprised. Her impatience made him cocky.

"My man at the Underground." He blurted and bounced with a confidence that perplexed The King.

Josephine held her stance. She stood steadfast, knowing now who his man was.

He used to be her man.

"He said some things, I heard some things," the dolt driveled and drained. He jerked his head and he glanced from left to right and slicked back unruly strands as he continued, "The gist of it is, little lady, he wants you back. And I have come here to bring you to him." He pointed his long, bony finger at her and his narrow face followed, getting dangerously close to her bite. His visit had suddenly taken a personal turn.

He was very pleased with himself indeed. He decided right then and there to add another task to the to-do list he was given. Maybe he'd like a taste of this sweet thing before getting rid of her? Maybe he wanted to know what all the fuss was about? The Boss would never know. It would be their little secret, his and Josephine's.

This nitwit obviously didn't know her real story. He only knew the fabled love job The Monster was working. Josephine could almost hear the pages the failed murderer was reciting to anybody who'd listen. She knew what he was leaving out of the crooked tale and what foul scabs he was filling it in with.

This Converter had just given her another flagstone for the path that was going to lead her and the boys safely back home.

She gathered all the pieces and placed them in their proper order.

So The Monster had built himself a new hiding place, had he? The Underground, is it? Josephine could see it perfectly. Black punk plywood and jukeboxed, mud-soaked enough to keep the better out. It had a grand amount of space and it was purposely cavernous and echoing. Oh, and lots of core music hooks for minnow bait.

This thing had no doubt revealed her whereabouts to The Monster, of that she was sure. She pushed down the jumps in her stomach with heavy air and collected herself quickly.

The lines were now drawn. The war had officially begun.

Josephine had almost forgotten the presence of Joseph the Converter until he tried a shoddy repenter's lecture on her. For some reason, he so wanted to be heard.

He was the typical Monster flunky.

Josephine did hear, oh, maybe every eighth word. His sermon ended with the same kind of thud all the preachy gobs drop. She yawned like a lion. She was becoming impatient and bored.

Josephine took a very slow step forward and proceeded to walk past Joseph. She brushed softly by and turned into his back. She was very close.

He was intoxicated by her warmth and a little alarmed. He suddenly became very aware he was in her church and Josephine's religion was lifted from another kind of bible he'd never cracked. He would've trembled if he weren't so stiff.

Josephine felt the bulge she was seeking. Hardened steel, an expensive blade placed cheaply on his person between the crack of a sorry novice who was in way over his head.

He reached back for her without turning and she avoided his hand easily.

"What are you afraid of, Miss Josephine?"

He dared ask her such a thing and she dared answer the fool.

"Everything," she cooed. "I couldn't be this brave if I wasn't so frightened."

She paused the perfect amount of moments.

Then it came again. Her voice, so rare to the air it was.

"Hush, boy, please. I'm so very tired, tonight."

She wrapped her arms around his waist.

It was so unexpected.

He felt her on his back, her soft waves of joy. He held her hands just above his belt. She laid her head between his blades and closed her eyes and sighed.

He felt peace. He did, he felt it. Just like the calm that Jesus promised him, only He could never deliver it like this. She was rescuing him, wasn't she? She had chosen him special.

No words, no sounds passed between them. This moment took him for everything he owned; everything he stood for was never invented until now.

Now he existed.

Josephine gave him silence so he might hear his own voice again.

So he might hear his own last words.

One hand pulled from his, the knife gently lifted and properly plunged back into Joseph, business end first. She felt the crumple begin.

His eyes opened wide and he learned too late what all the fuss was about indeed.

Joseph's last words were not unheard.

The Monster's name was finally confessed and Josephine was the only one close enough to make it out.

Joseph wasn't coming back and neither was she. Not yet.

Chapter 18

The Unholy Trinity

It was a collision of crime, stars and joy.

The Saint, he had a pace on. He knew Josephine was still beating and battling. He knew she was waiting for her time. He knew she still beat for him. He just knew it. He had to.

What he didn't know was that he had a beautiful moonfaced boy. He dared not hope such a thing but every now and then he wished hard for him.

He had to assume the worst. He had to believe his son didn't survive the attack. He wept storms constantly and couldn't keep the rain from drowning his insides.

The Saint's pace thickened.

He'd pelted a ditch in the back yard with his wingtips and he cursed the gods over and over. He cried some more when nobody could see.

The Saint wanted his woman in his arms. He wanted Sun Son deep inside their embrace.

He wanted his family back where he could protect them.

This kind of waiting should've never been invented.

The Monster had some wishful thinking going on, too. Hopefully, he had thought, the animals ate what was left. Wistfully, he prayed to a god of rationalization that would let him know he did the right thing by himself, he, the one who deserves everything for nothing, The Entitled One.

Unfortunately he'd caught a low desert wind of Josephine's most mystical skill of survival.

He could feel the rumor of her, the presence of something wild. He brushed it away as quickly as he breathed it.

The whipper he'd sent to finish the job, if indeed there was one, hadn't returned. He convinced himself that after finding no evidence of Josephine, the grifter skiffed a cowardly boot dance all the way back to wherever it was he came from with the half cash still padding his pocket. The Monster assured his weary soul she was indeed gone for good and sometimes late at night, lying on his dusty bed tucked far inside The Underground, he believed that bedtime story.

The Monster was as deeply hidden as Josephine. The difference was the camouflage.

He thought he was safe.

Josephine knew that she wasn't.

That was her backward advantage.

It hammered down on a different kind of armor. It molded a pointy breastplate that shot out good and far in front of her overtaxed heart.

Josephine knew the battle was inevitable. She knew there was an angry shadow following the accidental trio.

This entity was indeed The Unholy Trinity. Each touched at the points and shot out toward the other. It was an exhausting triangle.

The Saint waited for a sign.

Josephine waited to give it.

The Monster waited for nothing.

Chapter 19

Pieces of Grief

Dennis Bullock was officially worn out. He ran his woody hands through his sandy brown mop that had somehow grown out to a seventies long in a very short time. He rubbed his salty beard and squinted his story lines down hard.

June, his youngest climbed up him like he was just another ragged tree and rubbed her blazing curls against his cheek.

"C'mon Daddy, let's go on the swing." She demanded it with patience and he obliged the little bossy without argument.

As the weary detective pushed the very serious swinger he went over the sharper points of the tale of Josephine.

Instinctively, he knew volumes about the little lady but the actual facts he'd uncovered wouldn't plaster a post-it.

He needed more.

He shook off the furrowed trance to find June still happily being pushed on the swing by her father.

His youngest was only three when her mother passed. Wanda was five and their oldest, Dolly, was seven. They'd been introduced to the worst kind of thievery well before they rang in their first and most innocent decade. Bullock's anger rose to the back of his neck and he heated like it happened yesterday.

He hated the fear of having something to lose. He was not comfortable being papa-vulnerable, that's why he became a cop in the first place. It made him feel like he had some control over the constant and looming evil that hovered like wet smoke over us all.

Bullock knew deep down nothing could've stopped the monster that stopped his Tracy, just like he knew nothing could halt a man in agony from seeking the hollow relief of revenge.

The detective had found bits of The Thief floating in the halo of blood that surrounded his wife's body. There were black hairs and skin under her nails. Footprints were pressed and stenciled to reveal pointy, low-heeled roach stompers, possibly worn to compensate for a short stature. The glaze of a possible pompadour was slimed all over the alley wall. Bullock could still smell the cheap scent of Tres Flores as he walked past the yellow tape. It was the preferred pomade of the south side Billy's that cruised 3rd in Pomona. The detective had gone over every detail, every bitter twist and tangle, letting it naturally exaggerate its significance until it grew gigantic.

Even magnified, he still couldn't make out a face.

Chapter 20

Josephine's Black Knight Beauties

Have you ever believed in something so much that it actually starts to revolve? It erupts and turns and starts to grow things, breathing, heaving and evolving things? Have you ever had a conviction so spiked, so hammered in that it conjures up its very own sun and moon, spitting them high into the fresh, ever-loving sky?

Josephine did.

She could make something out of nothing.

And like all creations, mutations are sure to twist up and out of the fertile new ground as well, howling and thrashing about like raw beings usually do.

The Black Knight Beauties, buds bursting, stems thickening, bloomed a color never before seen on this new frontier. Josephine's seed had become so potent, her sin of creation could occur without consummation. A new danger was born.

Their doctrine stated they'd begin with their own savages. When their very own boneholders were properly pierced and emptied they'd move on to less selfish endeavors.

Only then would they consult the screaming newsies and silent stories printed, rolling and perfectly ignored on both screens and porches. They'd each present a page they found worthy and the judge and jury would rise from their familiar hearts, deciding whether to brighten or fade The Monster's guilty glow.

Cloaked in the invisible with a smash of lipstick across their smack, they'd open it all up and turn it inside out. They'd march toward the yowls and follow the scabby trails. They'd listen. They'd hear the unheard and speak the unspeakable language they all understood but never wanted to tongue.

They assembled at night like they thought they should, like they thought she'd want them to.

They dressed in the same bootcut Levi's and white tee, same square-toed black engineer boots, common and sturdy and most certainly inspired by their crashing King. They pretended it was her skin stretched over their skeletons, her burden bursting through the ceremonial threads of the working class.

From a lost moment they'd found their nerve. Just like her.

Just like Josephine.

The rumor of a woman vigilante, a survivor King trying to reclaim her birthright, had leaked from the inside of The Lost Chambers and had seeped a stain onto this needful group. It was most likely dripped from a Pennybride's pout, a bored and noisy one at that. Her tittered tale of a brutal beauty with a fatal temper had indeed intoxicated this litter of kittens. The chatty Bride had brewed a potent new wine and toasted it in Josephine's name, tapping the once-empty goblets of this thirsty pack. To The Outlaw King, our wicked, wicked Savior!

Josephine's tale had indeed swished softly over their open sores like a healing and magic wand. Funny how gods are born.

Bullock had whiffed a bit of that gossipy air as well. He'd been keeping his ear to the 1 percenter's flaky asphalt road and could almost feel the beating breath of the three-patch poets telling of a woman made wise to the ways of the world against her will. The detective had also heard of a mutation, a breeding of sorts that had sprung up around the edges of the dusty outskirts surrounding their Inland Empire.

It seemed that a group of slightly conspicuous women shared the same kind of fatigue and resolution as the rumored, willowy pinup ghost.

There were a few hide-aways mentioned but one more than any other.

Bullock started there.

The women had set to meeting in a blackwashed biker bar owned by two saucy sisters, both named Marie, after the blessed virgin, of course. The siblings had a nice little business floating out there on that sea of sand and they kept themselves from sinking by keeping their holes closed.

Red Marie and Blue Marie welcomed all gals, crossed and straight and even the fellas as long as they were desert gents.

Many courts were held inside The Two Maries Saloon but none quite as fatal as that of The Black Knight Beauties.

The gang enjoyed the feeling of Josephine rumbling roars in their chests, a snarl that growled with a grand purpose.

The same purpose they positively believed was Josephine's as well.

They imagined the humble crown, the comfortable throne, both modest at best that belonged to their King and they vowed loyalty to all that it meant, all that it stood for.

The Beauties didn't know Josephine the woman, the breathing, seething, complicated thing that stalked and walked the stomp of the living dead. Very few did.

She was excruciatingly human.

Josephine was nobody's god.

The Beauties refused to let any other possibility or reason for Josephine's cutting deeds land. They had discovered flight with her dark legend, and their new wings flapped loose and wild now. They never wanted the nosedive of their King's temper to bring them down. No heavy flaws allowed. This was their perfect loyalty and it was weightless.

Their retelling of the tale defended Josephine's vocation and became more and more holy with every recitation. They blamed the lambs, you see. They were cocksure the oily things had subconsciously turned themselves in and laid their guilty necks before her, offering up their jugular like a whip of sacrificial licorice.

The Beauties stomped in unison and pledged to fight battles lost by the weaker and less fortunate. The road to serve felt good. It felt right, solid and even.

And so on this decidedly righteous night, they all hailed Josephine before this, their first act of imitation in its grandest form.

To The Outlaw King!

To our Josephine!

Chapter 21

Frieda's Sin

So the minutes read on this dusty warm evening, ticking off in a smothered tocker deep inside The Two Maries Saloon.

What would our Josephine do?

That was their second question.

The first?

"Who's it going to be?"

On this night, the sect of six decided that one of them was indeed more dented and desperate. One of their soldiers seemed to be sinking faster and deeper into the woe than the rest of the scarred sallies. This one needed a healthy hand, strong and quick.

Annabelle, the statuesque pale raven and founder of The Black Knight Beauties throned the narrow end of the wood-slabbed table and leaned into the group. Her blue eyes settled into the six pairs that looked upon her, weighing their want and their need.

She nodded past Bobbie and Cilla. Their Monsters could wait. They were the gang's most recent members and their wounds were still a bit too fresh.

She then waved Dorothy's and Edith's agony gently away and reassured them they were very close to next, with a reassuring touch to their forearms.

Her eyes then fell sympathetically on their quietest and most desperate member. All of their motherly gazes followed Annabelle's and the fatigued soldier raised her weary head in hope.

With that the decision was made: Their first deed would bring down the devil of Frieda.

Frieda was thirty-four and sugar cookie sweet. She had a soft and curly sadness surrounding that round face of hers. You couldn't avoid the sinking once you fell into those night-ocean eyes. And she'd keep you there until you saw what she saw, felt what she felt. Her grip of a gaze would hold you down until you witnessed the crime of her heartbreak. She'd fill you in without so much as a peep from her baby pout.

Lately, Frieda's sigh had deepened, creating a deafening echo of hurt. Her clock had indeed struck its last digit; her bomb was heated and lit.

Before tonight the flock was little more than a griever's gathering, a place to unfold safely and discreetly. With their red-ribbon tales of a true King they'd become a new race of beings, an unsettled set of something never before born. Their newness stung but did not dissuade. They had their star and nothing could dim it.

The Beauties would set a time and hide their rides behind rocks and dunes that were long forgotten. They'd stride past the regulars, never raising an eyebrow or a second glance.

They'd give a double-nod to the two Maries behind the bar and seat themselves horseshoe-like around one of the rectangles in the back.

They were very familiar with the crime against their fellow soldier and they were well versed in the comings and goings of the monster they were about to slay.

Her name was Tania.

She was born without a left pinky and a right conscience. She was pointedly crude, an impeccable liar and in spite of all that, was loved completely by the young mother she called Freedy.

Tania wasn't all that interested in the waitress that served her almost daily at Billy's Diner. It wasn't until Frieda began talking about the daughter she was raising alone that she became suddenly attracted to the young mother and her single situation.

Tania had very specific needs and this dumb and broken thing was just what the soulless vulture ordered.

She'd sit in Frieda's station from then on, courting and charming her with tales of taking over her loneliness and replacing it with a real family. She promised days peppered with posies and kisses and nights forever salted with the sultry.

Nothing would ever taste the same in their home.

But that's not how it turned out. Tania went out every night, leaving Frieda shaken and stirred and emptier then she'd ever been.

Tania paid less and less attention to Frieda and become almost obsessed with Frieda's daughter, Pearl.

Frieda was an effective wall between the two until Tania came home one night very drunk and very driven. She backhanded the young mother who was out before she hit the floor. Tania made her way to the little girl still sleeping. True darkness filled Pearl's room as the monster shut the door behind her.

Frieda awoke to find Tania gone and her baby terrified and touched, cursed with a grown-up knowing way before her time. The guilt of letting everything get this far consumed Frieda and she caved hard and deep, leaving not an inch for a single breath of forgiveness for herself. She was suffocating.

Tania was the cruelest kind of killer, the half-murdering kind that takes the blushing pink innocence of a child while leaving only a fatal black memory that could smother any and all joy every babe's entitled to.

Best to rid us of the cause, to send her soul crashing backwards, reversing her bad birth.

The Black Knight Beauties stood and Annabelle, bowing toward her fellow soldiers whispered, "Let the fault of this fall like gravel on us all."

Chapter 22

Her Daughter's Mother

Frieda tucked a park about a mile from Angel's Roadhouse. This was Tania's favorite free ride, all the pie and pool she could down as long as her fight was potent and her reputation remained effective.

Frieda recognized her silhouette from the entrance and she watched as her monster sauntered around the table like she invented the felted game. Tania was tall, just over six feet and she owned every inch of it.

Her squinty gaze and crooked smile only added to the beer-buzzed onlookers' intoxication. Her black pompadour, always meticulously ducked, bobbed a curl just over an ice-blue eye as she made yet another perfect shot.

Back in the day, Frieda remembered hitting a bit below Tania's chin where she could suck the promises and swallow them with just a tilt and a pouring. She recalled the scent of Blue and how its essence turned sweet when Tania warmed.

Then she remembered her daughter and nothing about the strut or the stride of this woman held any power over her. The Tania she'd loved so fully had deflated and much to her surprise had become quite small and manageable.

Frieda checked her back for the shiny sharp and ran a slight slit down her thumb to make sure it was working properly.

She felt incredibly calm and for the first time in her life not only knew who she was but who she wasn't.

She was not Tania's victim or anybody else's. Frieda was simply her daughter's mother and she was going to earn that title back by doing the one thing every mama does well: She was going to keep the monster away.

Frieda's stroll was graced by a new kind of god, a silent and immediate one. It lifted her through the room unnoticed and she landed in front of her unattended creature.

A soft gaze came across her newfound face of fake and it teetered Tania a bit. This was the stained glass window of hope she'd imagined since the day Frieda had left her. She always knew she'd come back to her.

Tania helloed Frieda as if only a few dark minutes had passed since their last encounter. It was insulting but expected. Tania had the ego of a bloated and entitled dictator and she hadn't changed, not one bit. But Frieda had.

Sink into my fake smile, Beast. Sink deep and fast and don't take a breath down with you. Drown in the image of yourself reflecting in the blackest pools of my eyes.

Nothing could stop the Black Knight Beauty from this necessary task, not a look, scent, touch or feel.

Frieda leaned in a bit closer and examined what was soon to be destroyed. She said nothing to her monster for the longest second.

Then, very softly and too simply she mouthed, "Good-bye."

It was easy and the cut was quick. Face to face, across the throat it slid. She wasn't ready for the rubbery tug of her monster's neck but nothing could stall the blade or the hand that pressed it past the pulsing.

Tania jigged and pumped it all out. Frieda waited. It was pretty fast. Tania stared up at her creator for the first time seeing the black mirror eyes that now held the true reflection of what she was.

Frieda laid the beast down gently, wiped the cutter on the green felt and tucked it back where it came from. She floated out the back and walked upright for the first time in a very long time.

A mother's courage found a new home in a young hero called Frieda.

Chapter 23

The Tattling Light on Darkness

Josephine's paper seemed downright violated that hot and furious morning as she came across the appearance of a story filling the space that was usually saved for her battles.

There it was: splattered in the local section, a true tale that seemed too familiar. The circumstance of steel against skin wasn't new but it was rare around here.

Was she becoming paranoid or was it just good old-fashioned fear finally knocking at her thick skull? Josephine couldn't be sure but something was definitely familiar.

The reporting of the wasting waltz had an essence that seemed brutally soft like a whiff of fresh perfume wafting from the corpse.

Josephine sighed the big sigh of impatience and smacked the black-and-white down with a spank. Nothing was ever simple.

The Saint was also a subscriber to the local tell. He poured over the crime section every day, looking for some sign of a repeat from his favorite offender. Surely The Monster would strike more than once? It's almost certain he was feeling omnipotent from the success of his perfect absence. The Monster would try his ghost again and The Saint would be waiting and watching, combing the morning ledger and consulting his simple wristpiece. He was a very patient man.

Bullock's desk was becoming a mess of biblical proportions.

The sixth commandment was cut up and tossed like confetti, littering the normally immaculate, silver steel tabletop.

It seemed another collar had met a razor. Bullock had gone to the wrong bar that night. He grew agitated and questioned his instincts.

Josephine wondered if the light was indeed tattling on the darkness. Only then would she roll her suspicion down to the place where the stains still seeped. The Lincoln needed a cool and healthy spin anyway.

After the boys were all tucked in, Baby Dagger shafted a stiffened soldier stance and stationed herself directly in front of Golden Boys' door. Josephine gave a nod and was off.

Chapter 24

Deep in The Posy's Bud

The Two Maries Saloon stood off the side of an unpaved road in Pioneertown. It had a horse stable and an artists' colony of sorts. This was one of those bars that always seemed to round up its unruly herd of regulars nightly with the call of some local Americana torching and twanging. After a little strumming and a lot of swinging, the loose noise would start a stampede of answers to most of Josephine's unasked questions.

She pulled over just ahead of the parking lot across the road and stashed herself nicely behind a rogue street lamp.

One thing about this desert: you can only see what the lighters want you to see. Anything without a shine fades back to the black. The headlights were turned off a half a mile ago and the spotlights that pointed to the tipped cocktail signboard illuminated the doorway.

She leaned against the Lincoln's thick door and sunk perfectly into its dim.

Arms folded, right stem over left, Josephine watched the show from across the street. The parade produced a line starting at cowpunk and smearing all the way down to goth.

And a beautiful line it was.

Finally, something disturbed the smoky stream. A gang of sorts with twelve oily polished boots bouncing with a new and fresh swagger. Their bop gave them away and The King pricked up her ears and sharpened her vision.

Josephine cocked her head. She didn't recognize any of their faces. She was a bit perplexed, wondering what her connection to them might be. Her squint focused fiercely and she caught a glimpse of the glamour they were copping.

There were six of them with the boots, the Levi's and the white tees. They came in all sizes of lovely but one thing stood out as the confirmation Josephine was looking for: the regal reflection of a matte red-mouth smacking the same nine letters from their pouts.

They all dripped "Josephine."

Josephine watched the march and slowly lifted her lean.

She didn't realize she'd been sharing the same shadows. Bullock had finally hit a timely mark and he stuck deep inside his blackened target until the seventh pair of boots crossed the creaky doorjamb of The Two Maries saloon.

He stayed far enough behind and suddenly felt very grateful for being so sandy blonde and unremarkable.

Josephine sauntered straight to the raw wood mouth of it all. The door girl nodded her in and let her pass. Josephine swayed right by the bar and glanced the two Maries. Their backs were to the belters while they argued over who would go home early.

She found a new lean on a blind wall and she blended back into the filth of it.

One thing the pack could not emulate was the sensitive instinct of a true royal.

They didn't feel the heavy presence of their King.

The secret six had already taken to gabbing and grabbing their cues, shooting their shots, pool and otherwise. They looked all tinted blue and glowy through the shadowy haze. Luminous.

Josephine tuned into their casual voices. She wasn't listening for a clue or an answer. She didn't really need to hear who their inspiration was or the why of it, she just wanted to watch them for a while, unnoticed and undisturbed.

Bullock was too far to hear anything but the bloody pouts were still visible from his corner of the bar. All seven of them.

It occurred to the detective that this was the first time he'd seen Josephine upright. She didn't look much bigger then when they spoke at the hospital but her presence was definitely taller than her sixty-two inches, sixty four in well-worn boot heels. He found it hard to look away from her. She gathered up nicely in the fitted jeans and t-shirt and he found himself enjoying the sight of her for as brief a moment as he allowed himself.

Josephine took in the lot. What to do with them was just as mysterious as what not to do with them and she shook it off, refusing to take on any more labor than she had to these days.

Josephine suddenly noticed there was a collective twitch in the pack. She employed the skill of stillness she had learned so quickly and so well once upon a time on the bloody desert sand.

She conjured a bit of a silhouette and leaked a shadow across their doorway.

They stopped their play like cubs do when Mama returns from the hunt.

All at once they turned to face their maker.

It was dark in that poolroom but there was no mistaking that outline with the curves, the square of the well-worn boot separated by the slight split up the legs, the hair falling upon the shoulders like a Veronica Lake curtain, the glint of the half-hazel gaze. Standing before them was their King.

They straightened and faced her wholly.

Josephine looked upon them. She lifted her chin a bit and took in the women that stood before her. She looked them up and down and back again. She tilted her head a bit and took a deep breath. She whiffed their sweetest agony, and the weariness of their fight perfumed the makeshift palace like some kind of heavy cologne.

After what seemed like an unholy amount of minutes, Josephine lowered her head and exhaled. She closed her eyes briefly and then opened them, never meeting their gaze again. Josephine turned on her worn and weary boot and walked slowly away.

The Beauties were afraid to move and they dared not follow the regal ghost. Bullock sank deep inside the gray and watched her pass.

By the time The Beauties found their nerve she was gone into the blackness of her desert.

They were left shaking, wondering what the visit meant.

They still breathed and none of them leaked from anything, not a hole or a slit was found anywhere. Confused but still inflated. That was all you could hope for after a visit like that.

Josephine blended back into her desert night proving it really was a part of her, always had been, always would be.

She knew her presence had more than jarred and awed the women. There were a lot of sideways glances and sputtering pauses back and forth but no real words fell from the borrowed cherry puckers. Josephine swiped her chin with the back of her hand. She slid inside that lovely Continental and inhaled the old leather, oil and smoke that so comforted her on these go-aways.

The Black Knight Beauties knew only one thing: That they'd landed smack dab in the middle of the truest rose, deep in the posy's bud and the essence of Josephine would live on forever inside of them.

Bullock slipped out as easily as he came in. He'd seen and heard enough. The red-lipped six with their low and airy whispers hadn't learned the how-to of the hush. He still could hear the syllables quite clearly: The Lost Chambers.

Chapter 25

An Almost Anonymous Man

The Daily Barker had a sandpaper roughness to it lately. Josephine's grip on the rag vibrated with trepidation. The uninvited heart pounds shook her narrow cage and she didn't like that.

She peeled back the smudgy headlines to reveal the real news buried deep inside the Local section. Another familiar story rose like rancid cream.

It claimed an almost anonymous man had been found pinned and pierced precisely. Almost anonymous, because some Betty obviously knew him well enough to leave her blade wagging in his flesh like a flag.

Josephine knew it was her scarlet-smacked six. Multiple stabbing jabs, seventeen to be exact, right through the blessed peaches. Yeah, that's the feminine aim all right.

Now he was just another drawer-filler until somebody claimed him but Josephine was pretty sure nobody waited for this man.

Since the meat target did indeed hang just below his giant belt buckle Josephine felt sure of something else as well: This man had taken something one of the ladies never meant to give up.

This was indeed the work of The Black Knight Beauties.

Josephine slowly put the paper down.

The Saint felt a warm rush of red come to his face as he read yet another story of a murdered man.

Something about the way he was taken down, the way he was described, he could almost smell the grease and gore. Something was going on, a revolt of sorts. How many stories like this had he read in the past few months? Josephine had few friends and followers but the ones she did have were loyal. Were they trying to suck the danger from the heated air and freeze her killer out?

What did they know that he didn't?

The Saint felt like he was losing his mind. How much more could he take? He rubbed his face with his hands and shook his head as if shaking off the crazy.

Josephine had fed her past to him in nibbles. He knew of her underground life and her deep desert acquaintances. The Saint was no angel himself and the darkness he owned gave him the insight he'd need to fill in the blurry blanks.

He wished he would've pressed further, a name or a place, something, anything at all that could help him with his night hunting. The Saint had nothing to lose.

He'd go to the places where these men were killed. He'd search the faces and creep inside their conversations.

Bullock had the same uneasiness and inclination as The Saint only he had access to the dead themselves. He opened the stainless steel drawer and assessed the damage of the latest case. He couldn't help but wince. Right in the peaches.

Was this the work of his mysterious little brunette and the mimicking six? It had been over a week since he'd witnessed their existence and he knew that somebody was going to end up lying on the cold silver with a sheet pulled neatly over their head sooner rather than later. Deep down he hoped it wouldn't be Josephine.

The thought took the detective by surprise. He wasn't prepared to care about anyone outside of his redheaded flock.

He took one last look at the dopey sap and covered his frozen grimace with the stiff cotton.

Chapter 26

Dorothy Bright

Dorothy was a pistol, a woman who knew the power of the rumble in her thunder. She enjoyed all of her little things in a big way and taught her children the trick of it. She'd woven a self-imposed leash and it never chafed or irritated her in the least. She was quite content in her radius.

Dorothy had weathered her share of ruining rain and sorrowful sun. She handled them gracefully as long as they wet and shined within fifteen miles of her three-bedroom, two-bath tract home.

She learned late that the storms down the way are a different kind of pummel and fry. She learned that lesson the hardest way.

Dorothy had taken a job at the bad-weather bar out of boredom. Her kids were grown and well out of the family home. She'd passed The Brown Fox so many times on the way to school, PTA meetings, grocery shopping and dancing lessons.

From the outside it had the look of a British pub but two steps inside the fake mahogany door and the across-the-pond charm all but dried up.

Dorothy had just the kind of shine they needed to buff their tarnished reputation and they welcomed her with a handshake and an apron. Neither was enough to umbrella the storm that was brewing.

A well-known stranger that frequented the place noticed Dorothy right away and summed up her soft parts in five seconds flat.

He spoke to her in the tender voice he only brought out for special occasions. He asked after her children and flattered her still-fit figure already ten years after forty.

In between beers he'd tip a smile and between pilfered shots, he'd wink. He'd try to catch her eye as much as possible and by the end of her shift he'd spill off his stool and ask for her full attention.

She went to the back to make a fresh pot of coffee like she always did. The scent of the deep brown always had a way of clearing the most stubborn of mists.

He followed her with a wavy kind of lumbering. It was an odd sway and he tried to hold himself up between tequila-and-whiskey whiskers.

He was tall and strong like an old construction worker, two-by-four arms, girder legs, and chimney head.

The cigarette machine stole his coin. Could Dorothy muster the smokes from the tin thief?

His speech had suddenly lost its splendor and quickly became cutting and short with a halting spit that blew out his face like a nail gun. Fwit pow. Fwit pow pow.

She'd done this task for him many times, nothing unusual there. She just had to snap the knob over and over until the captive smokes fell, that's all.

With her back to him she snapped away and so did he.

He grabbed her and shoved her face in the opposite corner of the tiny hallway.

He was in and out of her so fast, finishing with a snort of disgust. He threw the back of her skirt down and wiped his nose on his flannel sleeve.

Dorothy ran into the bathroom and vomited.

Where was this written? How'd this story get told? It was beyond her tears and too far away from her worries to even register.

Her fears had always surrounded the what-ifs of her family's safety. She never thought she was in any danger this close to home. She splashed her face and tried to rewrite the whole incident with a different ending.

She clenched her fists and pounded the porcelain bucket.

This was not her ending, nor was it her beginning or even the soft and creamy middle. This was not the proper telling of her tale at all.

She did the scrubbing-off and the jolting in and out of reason. She wondered the fault, the blame, and the bitter why and how. She questioned everything.

She'd been through bad weather but this was an altogether different kind of downpour. The real danger was not in the deafening thunder but in the quick and silent lightning.

Thereafter, Dorothy's absence did not go unnoticed, no indeed.

Frieda used to come in to see Gina during her lunch break a few times a week. Gina had been a waitress since their high school days and this place was a step up from the last cave. Gina had ended up exactly where she felt she should have. Frieda's visits were designed to teach her otherwise but Gina genuinely liked being a waitress. Frieda had to respect that.

Frieda had gotten to know Miss Dorothy in between serves and volleys and they hit it off immediately.

After missing her the last few drop-ins, she inquired as to her whereabouts. Gina only knew that she went out the back one night after setting a pot of coffee and never returned.

A pointed and knowing snort disturbed her delusion of privacy. She took her downward glance and pushed it straight into the skull of the dirty bear next to her.

Without turning he held the halfway smile until it hit the back of his worthless throat and slid down his filthy gullet.

Frieda blinked slowly and took in a deep breath. Her exhale made the perfect sound and she took her leave.

That identical knowing tripped off the alarm inside her as she set out to Dorothy's place.

She didn't know what she'd do or what she'd say to Miss Dorothy but somehow she knew she'd be welcome.

Months had passed, and Dorothy still grieved. It showed. The Stranger had taken a part of her that would never grow back.

She got angry. Then she just let all her mad settle into a fuzzy, floaty and wet melancholy like a heavy English fog.

The Beauties all knew that fog; the Knights were born from it. They had puddin' pie thickness in their identical knowing and from it a new and necessary bolt of their own brand of lightning.

The Stranger was mean, the plain and unmoving kind. His damage was a chain of bad breeding and it was obvious he had added a new kink to his links recently. The rusty noose was now complete and it shall be his only legacy.

Dorothy gave Frieda pieces of the pie little by little and Frieda dined patiently.

Dorothy confessed that she'd known he'd been watching her, watching her hair move as she let it grow longer just past her shoulders, watching her curves round out under the hip-loving apron.

Dorothy mistakenly believed his gaze would shoot past her fifty. She thought her number was the countdown to invisible. Frieda touched her hand softly and assured her she had no number and she meant it. Some women are always summery and even the dusty dullards are always attracted to her kind of season.

Somehow Frieda knew just how to comfort her and even heal her a bit. It was the most unselfish gift she'd ever given. And Frieda had one more present: an invitation to her very exclusive club.

Dorothy's winter was lifting.

Chapter 27

Annabelle's Calling

Josephine felt some kind of spiky hug that day. It embraced her like an inside-out studded straightjacket. She knew The Black Knight Beauties were up to something, she could just feel it.

It had been a few weeks since she'd read anything familiar. The absence of a perfume-soaked page floating its bloody fumes up toward her heaven made Josephine almost as nervous as the bone-dry black-and-white that lay low and silent on the Formica.

A following had to happen. It was going to be a long night.

Josephine bathed her boys like she did every evening. Between the giggling, the stories and the scrubbing she allowed herself to marvel at the soft miracle of her babies.

Sun Son definitely grew bones like his very large Da. The Monster was three over six and weighed five under two-eighty. That boy shone with all the right stuff and Josephine was smart enough to protect the glow from the stealing shadows. She sighed and remembered a time when his father had that same kind of shine.

Sweet baby Moonface wore his skin like The Saint but housed a bit of a temper like his Mama. His demands were quick and loud if not ministered to immediately and the humor of it made Sun Son and Josephine laugh the same laugh. That boy came into this world knowing how dangerous and dark it could be and was still brave enough to come out and bring his own special glow. Just like The Saint.

She finished with the singing and the reading and the listening and put them both in their beds. Baby Dagger took her place outside their door as her King slipped deep into that desert night.

Josephine caught a glimpse of her hair in the rearview and gave it a smoothing of approval. It curved a very nice wave over one eye without much coaxing.

The Lincoln kicked over to the oily purr she'd fallen in love with the moment she sat inside the dizzy beast. She inhaled and filled her lungs with longing. It was going to be one of those drives.

Josephine drove to the Beauties' hole and waited in her black spot.

The distance between them seemed too close for Josephine's comfort. The old haunts and happenings were just a few exits away and she wasn't ready for any kind of reveal yet. She sunk a bit lower into the leather.

Josephine was still bothered by the existence of the group. It lived and breathed for what? And why did tonight seem even more sinister?

She spotted the six and watched as they filled a baby-blue version of the Caddy she'd always wanted. She could hear their quiet all the way across the street.

She followed them as they took the Foothill Boulevard back way, a path frequented mostly by locals. It's part of the old Route 66 and Josephine had used it since her two-wheeled days on her beloved orange ten-speed.

After a few leading rights and misleading lefts, Josephine lost the Cadillac and cursed the arrogant distance she'd been keeping between the two classics. She wasn't worried though. She'd had a good idea where they might be headed.

The Beauties' boots landed purposefully and dug into the gravel, making a grinding sound as they marched toward their destination.

They were pumped and a little too proud of themselves, Annabelle even more so than the rest. She'd come up with this one all by her lonesome, just after the appearance of their King.

She'd convinced Bobbie, Cilla, Dorothy, Edith and Frieda that there was a purpose, a message in Josephine's visit and she was the one who recognized what The Outlaw King was trying to tell them.

Josephine drove into the familiar lot and hid her park as usual. She took a step outside the suicide ride and took a moment to compose herself.

Was this a curing trick for Josephine, the Beauties' own personal recipe for some kind of sinner-fixing medicine? Josephine didn't like anybody in on her healing. It was hers to pack with ice and heat, nobody else's. She knew the wounds and what they needed to close. She was not happy with this turn of events, no indeed.

Josephine knew the trails inside. She knew the dead ends and the never ends. She knew the paths that led to fine rooms of blended anonymity. She knew this place lined with old and new punkers and poseurs. She knew it all too well without ever setting foot inside.

This was The Monster's new hideaway, and it was exactly as she knew it would be, his new Underground where amongst these ruins he had decreed himself.

She made her way to the giant blue-steel door.

Chapter 28

The Beauties' Descent into the Underground

Annabelle led the Beauties inside where they blended in quite well with their Josephine uniforms, all spotless and unassuming. They felt a march coming on but not one of them let the stomp out. Still, there was a bit of a swagger in the way they made their way through the scratchy painted crowd.

The music pounded loud and fast like the pulses that typically pumped in these places. Nobody ever forgets their own rushing, the fast flow inside their bursting skin that can't get enough beats per minute, no matter how hard they stroke it. Proof that youth never ages.

Annabelle felt a filling calm as she passed the walls papered with stickers and Sharpie propaganda. She was cocksure of her calling and confident in her plan of execution.

The BKB's had never met the man they were after tonight but his story had been told with such detail that it had its own smell and taste. Annabelle's senses were prickly.

But it was his sound, the low and boisterous bray of a stubborn beastie that Frieda heard first. She tilted her untitled head toward the deep echo and the Beauties set out to find the source of the bottomless boom.

Annabelle knew the antechambers well. She'd practiced this place many times, and now she led the lethal Beauties swiftly toward the cavern that billowed with the Monster's final breaths.

It was Persephone Pennybride who introduced the book of Josephine to her younger sister, Annabelle. She'd cracked it open on visiting days like she wrote it herself and when she turned the blank, rumored pages the Beauties could've sworn they saw thick, indelible ink splashed all over her lap.

Persephone spoke of the giant Monster and his missteps that had tripped him into exile. She revealed what he'd done and how he'd done it, never realizing the power of the storied germ and how it would infect them all.

Persephone was just sharing a gab. It was her favorite pastime and she never thought she'd planted anything more than an amusing seed. She didn't give a thought to Annabelle's soil, still fertile with her own blood. The Persephones of this world never did know when to shut up.

The Beauties' descent ended with them just outside the black door of the most buried room in the Underground. They could feel The Monster sucking at the air around them.

With silent weapons gripped between their drips of red varnish, they slipped in without a knock or a tap.

The Monster looked up from his chair, annoyed. Girl bands could be so obviously ambitious and tonight he wasn't in the mood for any kind of pleading or pitch.

He rose to the full six three as he addressed Annabelle who was obviously the lead singer.

"Booking's closed. You want a show, send me an email." They barely blinked. The hate made rosy in their cheeks and the fear pushed heat down into their boots.
The Monster neither noticed nor cared.

"Go on now, get out. I'm busy," he said with an impatient growl.

Annabelle took a step toward him and gave him a show of the glint she'd been hiding in her lovely fist. The others emerged from the wall and flashed their loyalty to Annabelle and the mighty deed they were here to do.

Chapter 29

The Rules According to Josephine

Josephine checked the clock hanging above the ticket booth. It was too many ticks behind to be working. It's not like it could tell her if it was the right or wrong time to take herself deeper into the Underground, anyway. She decided to rely on her own sense of snapping it off.

Josephine knew what was going on. She realized it the moment she witnessed the Beauties' purposeful procession through the dank and the decibels. They were on a sacred mission.

Josephine found the back door, the only one open and unattended during a show. There was always one hidden entry in the back of these places and the only people who ever knew about it were landlords and ladies. Josephine had been both. She slipped through and found some welcoming shadows to duck into.

The music jerked hard and loud and it caught Josephine off guard. She'd given up the luxury of pity's ache long ago but suddenly she felt excruciatingly lonely skulking around the hemlines of the very subjects that once belonged and bowed to her.

She took in the old stances and glances. She peered out of the corners and hid among hung and hooded coats. She strained through the screaming chunks of guitars calling out memories she hadn't addressed in years.

Above it all she heard a familiar bellow.

It rang loud and banged against the walls thickened with old paint and silk-screened posters. She looked around to see if anyone else noticed the deafening howl.

Not one of the numb nocturnes turned toward the hollering. Their heads just kept on bobbing to the rhythm of the up-and-comers on stage.

The bawl had Josephine thumping inside her own skin. She needed to collect her thoughts and sharpen them to a point. What were the words cutting through the noise?

She couldn't make out anything, just muffled syllables oozing down the hallways.

A feminine yell was throwing out a fit of glee. Another one was chanting as she struck something that sounded like a sack filled with clay.

Josephine steeled herself.

The man's voice was answering, not with words but with guttural grunts.

The smell and the feel, the pound of the fury, it made the urgent rise up in Josephine. She waited for the drop.

The thud was more than loud. It cracked the cement like falling thunder.

Quickly she moved. Josephine's clock struck straight up her spine. She flung open the door. She spied the maidens at once, not so milky and not so fair. They silenced immediately and turned to face their King.

Annabelle still hovered over the hump, halting her final blow. Slowly she raised her eyes and let her face fall wide open with a pompous smile. To have her feat witnessed by its inspiration. Such an honor bestowed upon such a worthy soldier.

Annabelle rose and turned on the borrowed heel of a real and ripe sinner. She bowed her platinum head and whispered reverently, "Josephine."

The Outlaw King was not pleased with her. In a deep murmur, Josephine ordered the girl to rise and face her. The sound of her voice bubbled in their marrow.

Frieda gasped and put her red manicured hand to her blooded matte mouth.

They all held a collective breath as Annabelle did as she was told. She started a sentence and was stopped by the raised hand of the true royal.

Josephine inhaled and exhaled slowly as her eyes closed and opened. She breathed the air of disorder.

She looked at each one long enough to coax a shudder from their bat-filled fists. Josephine didn't do it to scare the uninvited admirers. There wasn't a spank around that could slap away the fixated loyalty of this gaggle. She focused on them because she didn't want to look at the heap that caused a need for a new emotion to stir inside of her soul.

Annabelle loomed above the still-heated, fleshy thing. Josephine waved her away and she took her place at the end of the line.

Josephine looked everywhere but down. She examined their wooded weapons. The dents most definitely snitched a clobber. She looked for red in the wood's grain and found less than a drip. Her temper began to vibrate within her.

Josephine slowly walked past the line.

She didn't need to look down to know who this Monster was.

This Monster was her Monster.

Finally, Josephine forced her attention to the injured giant. She didn't see the coward that tried to shoot her away that desert evening not so long ago.

She saw the face of Sun Son.

Josephine bent down and brushed the hair from The Monster's forehead. Suddenly she saw the one thing she thought his mama had killed in him a long time ago. Peace. It was that same calm Sun Son possessed so easily.

Something shifted deep inside The Outlaw King.

The Beauties watched intently the actions of their maker. Awe replaced fear as they witnessed Josephine's entire being changing shape right before their eyes.

In her softest voice Josephine spoke her unspoken rule:

"Somebody waits for him."

She said it low but it floated high above the decibels like the strongest of oxygen. The Black Knight Beauties sucked it in their next breath and their next.

"This is my oldest boy's father," she said touching the broken arm of the Monster. "You did not create this one. He is not yours to take! He is my creation and mine alone. If I see you come anywhere near him again, I'll be the last face you see."

Each one was given a gaze of foreboding excellence from the born royal, a gift they would hold in their hearts forever. It turned their blood to good and loyal blood, pumping finally in the right direction.

Josephine looked down at her Monster once more. He'd live, much to his dismay. His guilt had welcomed this beating and he was going to be disappointed at their failure to finish the job. It would not be her last look.

She stood up slowly like steam rising. The Beauties waited for their orders which were delivered as a look and nod toward the door. The Beauties borrowed the shadows Josephine used to carry her there and vanished into the still sweltering night.

Josephine's drive home was as hard and still as a clenched fist. She was different. Everything was different.

Chapter 30

The Cherry Vanilla Ghost

He awoke to a familiar scent, a perfume he never thought he'd whiff again.

The fragrance was soft and it swelled inside his chest when he inhaled. It lingered on his bruised cheek and bloody sleeve. She was there.

He rubbed his eyes and lifted his head to look around. They'd left nothing that even suggested they'd been there. If anything, they were a prudent pack.

At first he had thought they were just another desperate band looking for a gig at the infamous Underground. A second look brought him to a more sinister conclusion. They all sported a purposeful and similar style. With their throwback 1950s sensibilities atop a jean-and-tee uniform, these gals favored the working-class girls he grew up with and quite frankly, preferred. They didn't wear any kind of needy smile and they seemed far too organized to be musicians. He decided right then and there to surrender to whatever it was they came to do.

They descended upon him quickly and wielded old wooden bats over their lovely waves. He let them bring the things down hard, welcoming the long-overdue beating. He raised his arms to protect his head out of instinct but the rest of his breather was up for sacrifice.

The last thing he remembered was that blonde baring a blade.

All that hammering struck a mean bammy. His entire body bulged with aching. He stood up and the scent flooded through him again. The soft cherry vanilla wisps of it soothed him like they always had. He could almost feel her.

His train of thought was torqued and tumbling, but be certain: that was Josephine's natural bouquet. It was a perfect combination of everything she wore every single day. The comfort of her unique cuisine, it was even in the taste of her fantastic tongue. The Monster began to shake.

The music had stopped filling this place hours ago. Josephine had left him lying there in the filth he started so long ago. Why didn't she just do it, why didn't she just finish what they started?

Something circled. It wouldn't land. It was that scent. It was the shiny black, the dark, the red, the cellophane white skin, flashing and coursing through his pounding, dripping and angry tears. Against his face, they're a sin. He knew that. He got it. He inhaled deep, deeper no, deeper still. He held her in his lungs turning her back into his own blood.

He didn't understand. He'd killed, he'd abandoned, he'd lied and lay heavy because of it. Still, nothing dies if it doesn't really want to. Like his favorite fragrance.

So he waited, hoping nobody waited for him.

Chapter 31

Josephine Pays a Visit

Josephine had some tabs she was keeping, so many that they weighed down the well-worn pockets of her favorite pair of Levi's. She wondered if they jingled out her whereabouts, if they rang high and clear on those excruciatingly lonely nights she found herself wandering toward the shadows of her failed future. She cursed the selfishness of her longing and she swore each of these stolen visits would be her last.

Josephine drove to the edge of the view, the one they were to supposed to get lost in together, the one from the master bedroom of the house The Saint had built for her. She'd keep the perfect distance and pace the outer edge of the vacant black and she'd pretend she was inside, with the boys, with him. Then she'd scold herself over and over, slapping her palm to her forehead while whispering her apologies toward the two-storied Spanish-style tract home she had once teasingly called The Castle.

Sometimes she secretly hoped she'd make a mistake and accidentally beam the thinnest shaft of a blinding hazel up toward the bedroom window he was staring out of. It would flash in his face and illuminate hers. That would be the worst thing for him but it would feel so sweet to feel the weight of his gaze upon her again. It was such a selfish wish but she couldn't help herself. She missed him so bad.

Josephine had only been inside their home before it was finished, before the laying of the rich brown floors and before the painting of the soft-white walls.

She'd been to that window at least thirty times during their inspections, imagining what it would be like to actually live there. She knew exactly where that window went blind, where the natural fade turned opaque.

That's where she'd park. She'd follow his aching silhouette as it slipped in and out of the empty rooms, turning the lights on and off as he came and went. She'd shut her eyes tight and try to will a sort of time travel, a trip that would take her back to a day before her ears hung dead and deafened by the bang of deceit. It never worked. It only made her head hurt and it broke her heart past the mash all over again.

Sometimes she'd wait a small forever, watching that golden yellow square. She'd be rewarded with the exquisite shadow of The Saint passing and once she swore he saw her with a swift and pointy squint. But the hang of his head and the closing of the shutters proved otherwise.

Josephine would lean over the black beast's hood and palm her hands flat, warming them over the engine. She let her head drop between her blades and closed her eyes against the agony of the beautiful sight. She needed to leave but it was hard on this night. For some reason she couldn't pull away, something was holding her down, gesturing she take some kind of action.

But she was spent. She needed some dimes and nickels. No, some quarter memories to keep her thinking. She had no idea, no answer to the question being posed.

She thought of the first time they met and how her eyes couldn't meet his. He had smiled in a real way and that made her smile in a real way and it shied her.

Josephine had pulled at her tee shirt and tripped over her boots. She looked around the restaurant at anybody but him and drank more of the wine than was her custom.

She finally got the nerve to look up at him as he was walking her back to her car. He took her face in his hands and kissed her. He kissed her in a real way.

That crown came tumbling down with a heavy clanging, along with every stitch of rag she'd wrapped around that heart-shaped body.

Only God comes before the crown and as far as she was concerned, her savior had risen. Falling to her knees, the once and future King had whispered, "Hallelujah".

She swayed and swooned every time she thought of that kiss and all the kisses that followed.

She wasn't spent anymore.

She needed to send a message to his aching hollow. Something soft with a surprisingly tart slap about it, a smack that'll stick.

She twisted her hair around. She lifted it off of her neck. She let the warm evening blow on the back of it.

She smelled sweet cherry vanilla.

That was her answer.

In her purse she carried the source of that scent. A small bottle of secrets she mixed herself.

She found a porous desert stone about the size of an apricot and soaked it over.

The stuff sank into the granite swiftly. It was clear and slick and made a permanent pinkish stain in the sandy stone.

Josephine's bouquet made a permanent stain in a man's brain as well. She never meant it to. It's just how it was mixed. She made small recipes and always put the newest batch in the same bottle she'd used to swirl the first potion.

She then rubbed the stone between her fragrant hands and melted into the handy shadows that led up to the castle.

She placed the stone on the porch beneath the thorny leaves of the bougainvillea The Saint had planted especially for her after she'd mentioned her grandmother's home was lousy with the lovely hot-pink shrubs.

It was the hardest thing to do, to leave the gift and to leave but leave she did and as she ran back to the sleeping Lincoln she could barely see through the storm in her eyes.

She drove back to The Lost Chambers as fast as the beast could go and crawled into her cold, white bed.

She felt like she'd committed some kind of crime.

Chapter 32

Her Kingdom Awaits

There's only so much breaking a man can withstand. He crumbles with the interior smash-down that can only be mastered with practice. The Saint invented the wretched art form, sculpting from the inside out.

He looked out the window that should've held a picture of his family. They were supposed to be portrait safe inside the sacred frame they watched grow from wooden two-by-four skeleton into toasted stucco majesty. He held the keys to the Caddy, the one he kept revved and ready for its rightful owner. He steeled himself for another night of nothing but aiming at asphalt.

He melted down the stairs and faced the inside of the front door. He dreaded the opening of it. Nobody was ever there waiting on the other side.

He eased the handle click, swung it open silently and took in his usual defeated breath.

He nearly passed out.

He'd inhaled a ghost; a sweet-smelling, black-haired, white-skinned entity, and she filled his lungs like floating ether.

He walked into it leaving the door behind him ajar. He reeled inside of the heady scent, twirling and twisting, and he felt his heart suck in the broken shards.

It was she.

It was Josephine.

Was this some sort of wishful memory, some sort of voodoo trick?

He whipped around left and right, looking here and there, up and down.

He knew there'd be no vision, no fleshy flesh bouncing or bounding toward him but he now knew there was something solid left of her somewhere.

Josephine was out there struggling to find a way back in.

She was speaking to him in their language.

He looked out and smiled through hopeful tears.

He would wait there forever.

Chapter 33

Rosaline

The Trinity was restless. They felt struck as sparks shot out of their dark nowheres.

They sensed a collision coming on.

Josephine was having one of those days. Something was up somewhere. She prickled against it but she knew she couldn't stop the shake once the gritty shivering of it started.

The Monster was uneasy too. He couldn't get that smell out of his head, couldn't wring it out of his spongy, worthless memory. He raged against his own survival.

The Saint couldn't shake the essence, either. He thanked some fresh god for it. His hope felt like a new sun with new moons, new planets and new stars. A whole universe of shimmering sweet fate lay ahead. He was having a very different kind of day in his corner of the triangle.

Josephine leaned against her bar awaiting the Brides. It was time for the inspection and The King herself would take a sniff and a gander, deeming them acceptable for the evening's shift.

Josephine was growing bored with the whole routine and decided it was time to delegate this duty to Baby Dagger. Bee Dee could handle the whole place, Josephine trusted her that much. She decided this would be one of the last inspections she would perform. Josephine had more pressing matters to attend to.

She heard the click of the well-heeled lovelies and she turned to watch the fantastic procession. It never failed to satisfy her fancy hunger for beauty.

They stood before her straight and even. Josephine started her assessment from dark to light, petite to tall, getting most of what she needed in a breath and a glance.

The Brides wore deep red velvets, creamy whites and vintage brown blacks. The corsets worked a cinch that became less of a job the more they were employed. Josephine slipped her arm around the tiny waists and nodded. Good sturdy aching. She patted their behinds and moved on to the next and the next.

She stroked hands and turned toes. Josephine even made sure the perfumes were authentic. No copycats. She smoothed the waves and pinned the curls and ran her hands down their legs like she would a prize stallion, making sure the proper smooth had occurred.

She ended on Rosaline. She leaned in on her, inhaling the complete soul of a finished and fully grown woman. It was a healthy and silky scent she wore. Josephine had a different kind of relationship with Miss Rosaline, an admiration and respect she didn't have with the others. Rosaline wore white frills and flesh-toned stockings. Josephine was such a fan of her style. There was indeed a mutual worship going on. She nodded toward her knowing Rosaline needed nobody's approval, not even The King's.

Rosaline was fifty-nine years old. She happened upon The Chambers during one of her long and winding drives. It was just another stop she never meant to make, another place she never meant to go. The compound rose up from the horizon wearing the same colors as the land. It was a subtle distraction from the sand and asphalt scenery she'd been staring at for days. She pulled her gleaming white Fairlane into the already filled parking lot and stepped inside the strange world of the waiting. She ordered her usual, an Old Fashioned, and slid onto the barstool, feeling unexpectedly at home.

She was wearing white from head to foot; a smartly fitted pantsuit with a scarf she slithered off coolly, revealing a deep brunette coif Josephine would've worn herself.

As Rosaline settled in, Josephine watched a woman quite comfortable in her own skin, a stunning thing who knew herself well and owned a courage that came from having nothing left to lose. That behind-the-eyes melancholy was unmistakable and quite familiar to The Outlaw King.

Rosaline noticed Josephine too. She locked into the royal's faraway gaze, tipped her chin and gave her glass a lift toward the black-haired sister across the room.

Josephine rose from her throne and joined her.

The introduction was formal but the warmth of the handshake was actually quite soothing and casual to both women.

Josephine ordered a vanilla Stoli and Coke and engaged Rosaline in what was to be her most interesting exchange in months.

As they warmed their throats with their chosen charmers, Rosaline loosened her grip on the story of what became of her and the wonderful little world she'd lost.

Rosaline's life seemed to begin at seventeen when the enchanting young woman everybody called Rosie met the man of her innocent dreams. His name was Henry Winchell and he was born and raised in the Inland Empire, the only child of Stella and Monty Winchell. His family owned some modest but healthy lemon groves scattered throughout San Bernardino County, and the Winchells were known as one of the founding members of the working-class community that helped build this kingdom.

Rosaline's father was foreman at the steel mill and her mother stayed at home to keep an eye on Rosaline and her sister. They liked Henry immediately.

The twenty-year-old Henry rechristened his lovely bride "Rosaline" and they married the same year she turned eighteen. The newlyweds set up house in a small town just north of the 10 freeway and just a bit south of her parents. Back then it was simply called Cucamonga.

Rosaline took a job as a cashier at a local pharmacy called Gemmel's, a little store down Foothill, the boulevard formerly known as Route 66. She wore chic sweaters and pencil skirts and she charmed the customers naturally with her soft voice and warm demeanor.

Josephine knew Gemmel's well and nodded knowingly as Rosaline spoke of the ample penny candy section famous to all the local children. Josephine confessed to stealing a jawbreaker or four while waiting for her mother to purchase the dainty toiletries she so loved.

Rosaline tossed back her wavy main and let out a luxurious laugh, saying she thought she'd recognized the dark haired little outlaw. She imagined the woman in front of her trying to hide her pink cheeks filled like a chipmunk's with pilfered confections. Josephine let out a giggle and covered her large smile with a white hand.

Josephine noticed the tone of Rosaline's story revealed a rare gratitude and appreciation for what she had with Henry. They were simply, a happy couple, content in what they had and committed to the sweet struggle of keeping it sacred. They knew love and never took it for granted. Josephine sucked in every word and detail, carving them into her tablets and scratching them good and deep so she'd never forget what she too was striving for. She hoped the tale would leave a clue, something, anything The King could use to get back to her family. She leaned in closer as the details unfolded.

Rosaline and Henry were born and raised blue-collar folk and they kept to the same patterns that worked for their parents and their parents' parents. They would leave at the same time each morning, she in flesh-colored stockings and pumps, he in a modest suit perfect for his position at the Sunkist plant. Rosaline would kiss his lips and wipe the lipstick while straightening his tie. Henry would brush her pale cheek with his hand and give her the look that always meant the same thing: let's go back to bed. She'd push him off with a blush and a smile and he'd pat her sweet behind as she walked to the car.

Henry was a hard worker, a smart worker, and he was always thinking of ways to improve the plant's performance. That kind of thinking lifted him up from picker to plant manager within ten years, a position nobody expected him to rise to so quickly, but rise he did. Rosaline couldn't have been more proud of her husband.

Rosaline would arrive home by three, Henry at five, and she'd have a cocktail and dinner ready. The marriage of Mr. and Mrs. Winchell was indeed a charming thing.

The couple had no children but they had plenty of friends and family around to nurture and they took on the nieces and nephews as often as was allowed.

That is, until fate finally came to collect on all of their immaculate bliss.

It was November, the Winchells' thirtieth autumn together. The days had been ending in the usual fuzzy haze and the darkness was coming quicker and quicker to the clock. Henry was fifty years old this year and he still had the same boyish gait, still had the same thick head of hair, almost all gray now. He was even more handsome than the day Rosaline first laid eyes on him.

He was on his way home, home to his Rosaline, when he stopped to fill up the tank of the Ford Fairlane he'd bought them for their fifth anniversary. As he reached for his wallet a twitchy man approached him.

Rosaline dropped her head and paused in her story while her eyes filled and swelled. Josephine brought her back to the present with a touch and a soft squeeze of her hand. The agony was still wet and Josephine felt the dampness of her despair.

Rosaline said the twitchy man's name was Eddie and that's all anybody knew, really. He was a man who cared for nothing and nobody and wanted the whole world to fall into his bottomless pit. He didn't strike a pose or twist himself into a threatening posture. No, he was less potent and a complete surprise to her husband. He was never found and they'd stopped looking for the creep years ago.

Henry didn't witness the reach and he never saw the gun. He just took the bullet inside of him. It pinballed off of his gentle heart and out through his strong, supportive shoulder.

Josephine found herself tilting back her own tears. Rosaline's grief was contagious.

When Rosaline met the police officer at the door, she knew he'd brought the check for her fairy-tale life. Her happiness crumpled into bankruptcy and her heart suddenly didn't have a home.

She grabbed her pocketbook and keys and never looked back.

All Rosaline could do now was circle the perimeter of what used to be their wonderful life.

The Lost Chambers was just another crashing shoreline for Rosaline. Every orange evening after that she'd dock and flood a hotel, a diner or a bar with the weight of her weeping. She waited for nothing and nobody. Her destination had simply been erased.
Josephine held out her hand and offered her a bed. Rosaline wanted more. She wanted to belong, to this place, to this time and

to Josephine, if only for a little while. Rosaline didn't question the sudden need and neither did the former penny-candy thief.

Josephine nodded toward Baby Dagger and Rosaline was given the best room available in The Chambers.

Rosaline slept like she did on those nights when Henry was beside her. She felt a sweet interlude in this place, a break from the breaking. Rosaline had found a place to park.

Chapter 34

Nola the Quiet

It was a not a bad night for a Thursday. The bar was filled with wanting and the girls had brought their cinnamon kisses and ginger-snap lips. It wasn't the usual impatient, toe-tapping Thursday. It was a welcome step, one they could linger on and enjoy knowing tomorrow night's descent was everybody else's ticket to freedom. This night belonged to the ballsy boys and belles who had the guts to take it and they celebrated such bravery at the appropriately named bar called "Lucky's."

One of the later arrivals of this thick and generous evening seemed out of place. He strolled, leaned and leered like a regular, only Josephine was sure he'd never set foot inside her place before. She watched him window shop the divine and wondered if he could afford her heavenly wares. Something made Josephine's hairs on the back of her neck stand straight up.

He looked at each Bride and seemed like he was calculating something too deep for a romp, too involved for a tickle. He looked down too often as if he was contemplating something other than the usual business that took place in The Lost Chambers.

Josephine decided to stick around a little longer.

Finally, he chose Nola.

Nola was thirty-seven, a platinum-white hothead with cream-in-your-coffee skin. She wore black. Always. It mimicked her quiet darkness and matched her landscape perfectly.

Her garb worked like slaves against her bursting. She was extra-filled and bouncy, a pillow that strained the seams of the well-made underthings. Nola overflowed.

She came to Josephine by way of Tijuana. She arrived at The Chambers with the word "almost" scratched in her surface.

Josephine buffed her back to ready in less than a week and she swirled like a schoolgirl in the safety of her new home. Living without walls and ceilings in a town with no country, sharing no boundaries with convenient uncles and questionable cousins had made Nola a nervous girl. Having a room of her own now held her in the warmest clinch, a hug she never even knew existed. She worked and saved for her family's own safe and sound embrace.

Josephine watched the man take Nola by the elbow and lead her down the hall. She looked over the bar to make sure nothing needed her there and followed just as the bedroom door was closing.

This client was pure math. He wore a thin tie and a three-button suit, a cool pomp and worn and pointy creeps. His demeanor was as humorless as the zeroes he added to Nola's usual fee. He was an unsolved equation and for Josephine, he wasn't adding up.

Chapter 35

A Rip in the Blindfold

There was a miniscule rip, a seemingly benign tear in the filthy blindfold covering Nola's pitch-black, pie-pan gaze. She didn't give a squiggle or a squirm, not a kink or a jerk snapped the links of her serpentine twist. She just sat on the chair he'd tied her to with some sort of curtain clenching rope. She'd given up struggling a long time ago.

Nola kept stony still like a silky mannequin as she watched him prepare for her sacrifice.

He didn't know there was a slit. He didn't even check the kerchief once he'd cinched it around her satin waves. He seemed new to this profession, clumsily bumping off the furniture like a pinball, tripping over imaginary dents in the floorboards. Nola wondered silently if maybe this wasn't his true calling.

He kept mumbling off his checklist and cursing himself for taking so long. He was trying to get it right, to perfect the skills of his new occupation. He didn't care if she heard his bumblings as long as she couldn't see the obvious shortcomings of an amateur. But Nola could see, couldn't she? Through that tiny, insignificant rip she saw everything.

She watched him ready the dresser, placing the tools of his new trade in perfectly straight rows, arranging them by length, short to long. He set each sharp and shiny thing down carefully, wiping it across a piece of cheap purple satin he'd acquired for his budding business. It seemed pretty cliché, even to a simple girl like Nola.

Maybe it was an overly attentive mother or smothering auntie that had sold him a bill of goods he couldn't possibly live up to that gave him the phony strut he'd used to carry out this deed. Maybe it was an arrogant god that spoke to him through his fevered dreams of insecurity. Nola stopped thinking about the why and started considering the when.

He'd somehow convinced himself he was helpless to this calling. He turned and looked at Nola with her snowy hair and earthy skin. She was full like a woman should be, wearing her curves pinched and punched up exactly how he liked them. It was like she knew he was coming for her, like she was waiting for him all of her wasted life, he thought. Well I'm here now, sweet, sweet Nola. Your savior is here, darling.

Josephine could smell the asinine fear of a try-too-hard. It made her grumpy, antsy and tired all at the same time.

The happy couple had left all of seven and a half minutes ago and Josephine wondered just how misused those four hundred and fifty seconds were. Josephine lingered at the end of her hallway staring off into the center of her space, waiting for whatever bump or jolt was going to set this whole thing into motion.

She twisted her head and looked toward Nola's door. It was closed tight and the crack underneath wore dark. The camera in each room can never be covered but the lights can be out if the client so wishes, their own unbearable acts too much to take when they're illuminated. It makes for dusky shadows and rolling humps. If a hurting dance should occur, its tale would be told with the jagged outline of force. Funny how the absence of light creates the same silhouette no matter how clever you think you are. It tells the same story only inside out.

He was touching Nola with one fingertip, drawing it just outside the good parts, just around the details. Josephine could see the Bride was seated and somehow anchored. Patience, doll, just keep doing what you're doing.

Nola didn't shiver, didn't bump up, she didn't twitch or moan. She was silent and perfect. Stay smooth, sweetie, Mama's coming.

He kept saying the things he needed to hear from his own mouth, his god proclamations, his churchy preach climbing the mountain of threat only to tumble as a promise, a super sacred vow he was determined to keep.

The others. Well, they didn't behave so much and they weren't grateful for his presence like they should've been. That's why things had gotten so damn messy. His big finish left their once-smooth skin in tatters. He tore his slashes roughly and hesitated inside the nightmare of it, letting it splash slipshod all over the fabrics and walls.

Josephine didn't like the feeling, the face or the fake power of this blundering fool. His pace reeked of indecision and his hesitancy revealed the true novice that he was. She didn't like that nine minutes had passed and nothing rocked, nothing rolled and nothing rang out. She tapped her leather-wrapped ankle beneath her worn-out bootcuts. It was there, the shiny little sharp thing. She slid it out and up and its tiny "sneet" made her tall. She didn't bounce or swagger. No, this hall's journey was almost a kitten slither, all fuzzy fur and soft padding over the dark-stained floor. She stuck to the wall and listened all the way to the door. Josephine could make her breathing disappear just like that and that's just what she did now.

He was turning toward Nola still halfway sighted by the faulty blindfold. The slit only let her see what he was going to do to her moments too late. Nola didn't need the peek to know what was coming, she didn't need any magic voodoo mind read. She acquired her sharp intuition from a dull razor of experience and she knew this could be the inevitable ending to her story.

But somebody waited for Nola. Two girls and a boy slept with their grandmother while she worked for the home they lay inside of, safe and warm and far away from this kind peccadillo.

He was still talking in that rehearsed whisper, narrating his intentions as he readied for his ritual.

Through all of his rattle-tattle, Nola noticed something odd: She had stopped listening. She hadn't given up on her own true calling after all. Being a Bride was nothing to her, but being Mama, that was so something. Suddenly all of Nola's plans were made, all of her questions answered.

He lunged with a razor, almost twirling around her, grabbing the snow-white hair, pulling her head toward her latte spine. For the first time in a long time, she was present and very much aware of her pulse. She didn't scream, didn't flinch or resist, but she did indeed respond.

Nola, very deep and ever so softly, growled. She didn't even know she owned such a rumble, but there it was buzzing in and up her stretched throat. Her hands were still tied, her legs still bound to those of the chair. He was still talking, talking, talking, low and hysterical now. Nola found calm in the center of this storm and the trust of true presence gave her patience. She could feel Miss Josephine on the other side of the door.

Josephine clicked the handle and slipped in closing it behind her. She was in front of Nola, in front of him, such a lazy amateur, such an inept, wannabe villain. What an extremely successful fool. Nola stopped growling and let it stretch to her lovely grin. Even in the dark Josephine could see it and that red-rimmed smile of relief was returned with Josephine's twin crimson smirk.

It was starting to feel good in this room.

Josephine could see his blade was closer to Nola than hers was to him and she knew very well what a great distance that might turn out to be. He held it not like an extension of his hand but with the uncertain and shaky grip of a frightened boy.

He didn't lurch or slip when Josephine entered. He held fast to the pose he imagined he was holding in his head successfully and lifted his chin a bit in defiance toward the true Outlaw King. He thought the smirk Josephine had graciously bent was for him, a kind of nod or peck of admiration. He couldn't see the mocking grin Nola was sporting to her true ruler behind his bony back.

This deed had just gotten so much better, almost too much for the hack to handle. Cortez the Killer had his audience and he felt heated blood erupt from the filth of his toes to his simple, porous brainbone. Like granite, it was.

Until then he had no idea how much he desired a witness, somebody to finally see him, even in the dark.

Josephine was watching all right but he would get no applause from her small, pale hands, no hiss or boo would leave her ripping mouth.

Josephine felt her temper rise. She had to force herself to remember why she slipped into Nola's room. She didn't like the feeling of leaking control, of pushing the steel in anger.

She breathed in deep, letting the air connect her heart and head once more.

She was here to do what she was meant to do, to answer the true calling of a King.

"Did you come to witness my deed?" he asked coyly, almost like a schoolgirl. "Do you like to watch, Josephine?"

He addressed her with the familiarity of a family friend, letting the nine letters drip from his ridiculous mouth. It offended both of the women in the room.

She felt her temper heat back up to a boil and she blew it back down to a respectable simmer. She was getting good at this.

She took a very careful step forward. It made no stomp or click. The soft stride entered her into the lamp's vicinity and she summoned its illumination with a gentle click of the jagged wheel. Her face glowed in the half-light.

He forgot for a moment the position he was in. He forgot for one quick second what he was there to do as he stared into the eyes of a real noble. He could see now the blue blood pumping under the skin, shimmering with the immaculate truth of a born royal.

He knew then how ridiculous his voice sounded bouncing off the walls of a palace.

His humiliation made him panic and Josephine knew her presence had become too much for the brutal scene he'd prepared.

She watched all points that needed to be watched at once. It was a royal talent, indeed.

He cocked his head and tried to shake off his insecurity with a dry and hard press of the blade. He pulled Nola's head back exposing the lovely tawny neck; taunting Josephine with its inevitable opening. Nola didn't tick or sway, but a strange voice spilled from her throat, a hearty, girlish laugh.

Cortez became angry as man-children do and his movements became jerky and unpredictable. He slapped her to silence.

Josephine unfolded, inhaled and expanded.

He said out loud what he meant to do with that faulty blade and gave a rehearsed and borrowed reason.

Josephine's patience was at its end.

Chapter 36

Cortez the Killer

His name was Cortez.

Cortez the Killer. That's what he chanted every night before he slid his oily head onto his dirty, gray feather pillow. "I am Cortez. Cortez the Killer."

He liked the sound of it. It clicked off his overused tongue and gave his surname some rhyme and reason.

He'd say it over again in the morning too as he gripped his skinny black barber comb, slicking his greasy pomp into a perfect Billy.

He'd gaze into the chipped, leaded mirror and say, "Cortez, Cortez the Killer, I'm very pleased to make your acquaintance." He'd cock his head to the left, tilt his pointy chin upward and bear his bright white chiclets through a quivering Cheshire grin, all the while extending his insincere and delicate mitt toward nothing and no one. Then he'd lay the comb next to his straightedge razor, perfectly spaced and even, give a nod to his satisfied reflection and saunter out into the revealing light.

Cortez would imagine all sorts of brutal antics for that razor during his walk to work at the packing plant. It made the journey almost enjoyable as he happily slinked down the middle of downtown Pomona, keeping a solid strut all the way up Third Street.

The buildings of his city's center were tall enough to cast cold shadows and close enough to breed alleyways but nothing reached past the required stories needed to raise a skyscraper.

Still, Pomona held the evidence of more innocent beginnings with peeling murals brushed thick on used-brick walls, showing the purity of the orchard trade, growers and pickers standing shoulder to shoulder in front of the profitable citrus, as if they were partners and friends. Such a charming fable.

Cortez was born in a lemon grove, his mother giving birth to him next to a smudge pot. His father saw the stain and left soon after. Cortez carried his name first out of hope and then out of spite. He shoved his anger for him down with a bruising force like his father did his mother when he took the young girl's promise after a long day of crating. Cortez began to set his jaw as he stamped his timecard ten minutes too late.

He liked to imagine the blade brought to life magnificently by the brush of his grip.

The silver quick trails they'd slash as one true and powerful being always across some pale and sinewy neck making it ooze from its freshly cut ropes. Just the mere presence of its glint at the end of his arm could turn a mocking rant into a sincere and respectful begging.

Cortez did love that razor. It was the only thing his father left him besides the name and he used both to get back at the thing that created him.

The slitting task was a wonderful little job that made women surrender with a slump into his arms, falling silent and soft. She'd say nothing as he undraped her. She'd never protest his fondle, she'd never scream. She'd never flick his hand away either, which was the worst thing a girl could do to a man like Cortez.

The first one he brought to the red rain hop was a blunder, a thunderous mess. She was a bought-and-paid-for and she was more nothing than anyone he'd ever met. She should be honored to be the first dip of his fatal lead. For he was Cortez, Cortez the Killer!

It was the whore's fault the waltz never came. And maybe the blade, maybe it wasn't new enough. It dragged across her neck, making triangle tears as it bounced and skipped. It didn't slide and then slip away like it did in the movies he so loved to live in. It just sort of sputtered. He just left her laying in her own rent-a-bed and he spat on her chest as it heaved its last inhale. She, not Cortez had ruined their date.

The second one was met with a sharper blade and a higher bill was paid for her, so she almost looked okay. Not pinup perfect but she had the right figure. And this time he made sure the swipe was healthy. It slid right across, from ear to ear, but he didn't go deep enough and she began the death shake right in his arms. How dare she! It frightened Cortez; the mechanics of the flesh were so foreign to him. Still he was able to finish himself off after the rattling subsided. He was getting better. He felt pride in the improvement of his skill in such a short time. He was becoming an excellent partner.

He'd heard of The Lost Chambers one very hot and very loud Thursday night while waiting for a Psycho band to play. Cortez had been sitting next to a rather large and dapper Billy, close enough to smell his Tres Flores three months thick in his patent leather pomp. Cortez learned the secret location through drunken, clenched teeth and heaps of backslaps that stung with the weight of the stranger's meatpaw. Those would be the loosest and luckiest nine shots he ever bought.

The fabled road story the blowhard filled and spilled from his brag bag took Cortez straight to the magical destination. It was almost too easy.

For the next two weeks, he staked out The Lost Chambers. He watched the Pennybrides attend to themselves and each other. He knew right away which one was for him.

She was calendar girl perfection just like Miss October, his imaginary father's favorite month of the year.

He had the speech all ready. He wore the wardrobe and wreaked the smell. He was never more ready than he was that night.

They were all lined up and all of them one hundred percent as they should be. Like a garden seeded with all of his favorite blooms in all of his very favorite colors, flowering pure sin and sorrow all over the place. But there was only one bride for Cortez. Her name was Nola.

She was so beautiful and quite willing to go with him, even though he was such an obvious danger. That threw him a bit, but she looked so nice with her heavy curves all belted in and bursting out and he decided he could overlook her suicide tilt.

He offered his arm to her and hissed, "Let me introduce myself, Nola. I am Cortez."

Chapter 37

Bullock Amongst the Betties

The drive was easy, easier than he thought it would be. Straight up the 62 off the 10, past the Joshua's and the gothic rocks he sped.

The old Ford seemed to know this drive and Bullock could almost feel the pull of metal and fate leading him to some sort of liberating destination. It was the strangest feeling, the oddest ride.

Three structures rose up from the horizon and he could see it was a busy night at The Lost Chambers.

Bullock had heard a bit about these digs and he filled in the rest of its questionable details with his limber imagination. He had a pretty good idea what he'd find inside the middle one they called "Lucky's".

Bouncing Betties, booze and Billy's swimming inside the wood soaked palace. Bullock figured he'd wash up on their shore, uninvited as usual, and take the waves as they came.

He'd conjured up another wish as well: that he'd once again come face to face with the owner of this place, the woman they called Josephine. Josephine the Outlaw King.

The detective found his way to the thick and shiny center and ordered a Diet Coke with lime. When he lifted his sight he couldn't imagine the power of the vision before him.

It was a gathering of mixed matches and extreme divines. Nothing blended in and not one soul was faded. Everybody burned their primary's and they did it well and purposeful. Bullock felt like he was part of a panel in a graphic novel. He couldn't wait to turn the page.

But turn he did and there she stood.

Josephine.

She was wearing her embracing jeans and tee but she glowed in the low light like a painted saint candle from the grocery. She was okay being seen here and Bullock suddenly wanted to be seen by her.

But Josephine was pre-occupied with something down the hall. She didn't notice the detective staring holes in her skin and she didn't feel it either. She was there and then she was gone.

Bullock saw Josephine slip down the paneled tunnel and he wondered how close he could come in behind her without her knowing.

He slid off the stool and figured he'd find out the hard way.

Bullock saw the black boot heel tuck inside the door and he sucked the walls all the way to the sanded oak barrier, pressing against it like it was soft as clay. He planned on absorbing whatever lesson Josephine was teaching in there.

Bullock's fuel was his instinct and tonight he had a full tank. He could hear the bride and the "groom" but nothing came from Josephine's red mouth.

She was listening.

He would take her cue and do the same.

Chapter 38

Nolita Giggled

Nola couldn't shake the familiar, threatening chill this date was fostering in the deep and dead parts inside her. She was at once very weary and very awake. She walked ahead of him toward her room as if a pistol was piercing the small of her back. Something about him was pointing to the wrong.

That smell, the Tres Flores pomade this Cortez fellow dragged across his pomp, and the way he stood above her while seating her in the hardest chair in the room. All of it reminded her of her Uncle Tony, the monster that broke her when she was only six, the first of that side of the family to try a bit of the shy and sweet Nolita, as she was known back then.

The little girl had cried every time that thing came to babysit. Her mother shrugged it off. Nolita was just high-strung, that's all, overly attached to her mama. She'd come around.

Nola remembered how she used to pretend to be fast asleep when he arrived, and when that didn't work she taught herself the fine art of mind wandering. She'd visit all the wonderful and ticklish places a child's imagination conjures up when there's nowhere left to hide.

The weight of her uncle's visits had given the girl a burden's bend. She stopped looking into people's faces when they spoke and she said barely a word or two when they did engage her. Nolita was fading into something and someone else, the woman she called "Nola".

It was she who greeted the criminal when he showed up early dressed to the nines and ready for some kind of sick romance and it was also Nola who sat in the stiff chair waiting to take whatever it was this piece was dishing.

Nola was so much stronger than Nolita but the child made sure to never let her speak. When there was talking to be done, Nolita would make her way to the mouth they shared and leak in girlish tones as not to reveal the presence of her protector. As the years passed, Nola took up even more space inside the girl's tender places and Nolita found it harder and harder to keep the woman quiet.

By her thirteenth birthday, Nolita's "Nola" thought this whole ordeal had become tiresome and a bit silly. So hilarious to her, in fact, that sometimes she would even grin during the crime. So ridiculously hysterical was the offense to the growing Miss Nola that nobody noticed the child was becoming someone else entirely, an in-between thing that's never supposed to exist. Nola was now a permanent visitor in Nolita's skin and that skin was getting more ticklish with every unwanted embrace.

Nolita's uncle's scent, the one captured in his cheap and sticky hair grease always got to Nola. It made her shift inside the girl's rags as she tried to muffle the rising snickers.

And then one night it happened.

Nola giggled.

The Protector's voice was solid and full like a grown woman's and it echoed against the pink-and-white daisy wallpaper.

It made Nolita's uncle stop dead in the middle of the deed. He thought it came from somebody else; was there an intruder, a nosy witness? He looked down on the child's face. She was smiling. It wasn't Nolita's girly smile; no it was more of a sneering and cynical mask, the sort of expression that could push out such a haunting chuckle.

Nola looked him straight in the eyes and giggled again.

He slapped her hard with the back of his hand, trying to smack the girl back from this evil possession. The frightened monster watched her small hand cradle her burning cheek. Nola kept her gaze steady through the sting and said, "Get off the girl, Tio."

She spoke in a husky tone, nothing like Nolita's timid squeak at all. He launched himself off of her as though her skin were on fire.

"Get out," Nola growled.

Her uncle's eyes bulged and his mouth fell open. He pointed his finger at her and stammered out the ridiculous word, "Devil, devil!"

With that Nola threw her head back and laughed loud and long, slamming the girl's legs shut and standing her upright with a snap.

The coward screamed and ran out of the house, crossing himself and swearing at the same time. Nola gathered up all of Nolita's belongings and took the can of cash her mother stashed above the fridge. She left Tijuana that night and never returned.

Nola now possessed the girl completely. She went on to live a grown woman's life even though she was barely a teenager. She had the babies one right after another with a man she didn't love but liked immensely. When he passed, Nola took on the extra task of daddy. She had the babies and their father's mother to take care of, and The Lost Chambers gave her the most money for the least amount of time. It was a no-brainer for the professional survivor.

Nola's mind wandered back into the room with Josephine, the stranger and the chair. While he was binding her shins to the hearty walnut sticks it wasn't fear that she felt. Not even close.

Nola started to fill and harden as if being pushed from the inside out. Her spine straightened and lifted those curves like a forklift.

Her skin fevered and flushed and a hearty flow began to rise up to her mouth with air she hadn't used since she was a child.

It started with a low purr, the air rushing past the rough and unused parts, making it vibrate. As it rose it took on a rumbling and when it finally parted the pout it became a full-on growl.

Cortez turned on his two-inch heel, tearing his gaze away from Josephine and looked at the Bride.

Nola giggled and then she started to laugh, wild and uncontrolled like a can of cola cracked open after a million quakes of shaking. She started it all with a seeping hiss, bursting into a shooting spout of playful, girly guffaws.

Cortez was furious! She dared to laugh at him! She was going to pay and pay more than anyone has ever paid, he'd see to that! That laugh was going to be very expensive for this Pennybride named Nola.

Cortez grabbed her face and got as close as he possibly could.

"You think it's funny? You think I am funny?" He began to rear up and roar, slashing the air with the razor and shrieking.

"You are not my first! I wanted this to be special. Perfect. For you, Nola. All the practice, all the work. This was my gift to you."

He continued, shaking his head in disbelief and waving the blade between the two women.

"That redhead, what a mess, what a mess", he said swaying his head from side to side. "The blade, it wasn't even new! But for you, for YOU, I bought the best, the best Nola!"

In the hall, his ear burning against the hollow door, Bullock housed the echo of Cortez's confession and felt the over and over bounce of an agony never invented until now.

This thing had killed his love, his life. This flick of filth had taken his daughter's mother away from their still tiny and clinging fingers.

This foul coward had made fear and pain his wife's final knowing.

Bullock froze.

Josephine felt his cold stillness through the flimsy grain.

The Outlaw King had sensed Bullock's presence for weeks now. His shadow had sliced hers on more than one occasion but his darkness wasn't threatening. It was almost a comfort.

She eased a crack and peered at the face that was now snowy, even under the beard. She gave him her nod and he leaked into the angry room swiftly disturbing none of its madness.

Cortez didn't notice the intruder, he was too busy trying to regain control of the buzzing bride.

He raised his arm and crossed it over his thin frame with a lefty swing and backhanded the bound woman across the face.

The sound of the slap snapped the detective to life. He stood there thick, heavy, unmoving and unarmed.

Bullock shot a look at the King and with that one sorrowful glance she knew everything all at once. He would do what he was meant to do.

Josephine did an inside shiver and stepped aside.

Cortez leapt behind Nola.

The tiny man filled his grip with her platinum coif.

"You wanna watch, too? Yeah? You think you can stop me?"

Cortez was drenched in his own flop sweat, twitching and jerking and waving his weapon.

Everyone else remained as still and steady as polished marble. One buzz, one tick and this bomb would blow.

Josephine's heart bounced in her ribs with anticipation and she felt something she didn't quite expect: excitement. Her desire to step in and end this one was overwhelming and she had to stifle the pounce too many times.

But this was not her monster.

Bullock looked at Nola. At least the giggling had ceased.

Suddenly he saw the big eyes fluttering underneath the blindfold. Nolita was coming back to life.

The Pennybride burst out of the bounds so smooth and fast that Cortez didn't even feel her relieve him of his razor. She took a stance above the quivering monster, bearing the teeth of the borrowed blade.

Cortez fell on one knee and the beautiful Nolita brought him to the other, with the razor's edge pressed ever so lightly against the popping pulse in his neck.

A precious kneel, finally.

Nolita looked down on the sweating fiend and tipped her head in a familiar pose. Just like Mama, Josephine mused.

And just like Mama, Josephine reached for the hand courting the blade and pulled Nolita to her side.

Cortez looked at Josephine with pleading eyes. The King gave him a nod, not of mercy but one that assured him this was indeed his end although not by the hands of a woman like he'd prefer.

After all, he was not their monster.

Bullock lifted the blade from the Pennybride's grip and stood above the animal. Cortez felt fear and pride replacing the power and the lust. His hardness flattened and he fought acceptance of the relief the detective was offering.

Cortez used begging talk, maybe the kind of pleading his own sweet Tracy had tried.

It made him even smaller and cheaper, like tarnished and tossed loose change.

How many times had the husband dreamed of this moment? How many hours did the father waste picturing the drawing and quartering of the beast that left he and his family in a million pieces?

He'd not waste another second.

Bullock bent down low, all the way down to Cortez's greasy ear and smelled the stink that made his blood boil and burn to black. Tres Flores pomade.

Bullock's voice hissed through his clenched teeth into the ear of the first man he'd ever killed.

"Pray to me, boy, pray to me."

Cortez frantically searched his faulty recall, as if there was actually a prayer that could reverse the guilty's fate.

"Pray to me," Bullock repeated as he straightened up to his full seventy-six inches.

Cortez obeyed, clapping his shaking flippers together in a Catholic clam. He even managed a catechism bow of the head, his eyes still on Bullock.

Cortez started a whiny appeal but Bullock just didn't have those kinds of listens.

The father of June, Wanda and Dolly stepped slowly behind the monster, the thing that ripped their mother from their little arms. He laid his hand on the greasy patent-leather pomp and let his fingers grip the hair like a handle, forcing the beast to watch what had to be done.

The blade slid like a hot ice skate across his spindly neck. It didn't hesitate at all. Nice and new and sharp. Forgiving one might say. Whiskey quick, it was.

Cortez the Killer's eyes froze open, empty and brown like the rest of him. Bullock let himself fall into the lifeless gaze and allowed the blank stare to comfort him for one rare and selfish moment.

Nolita watched as Josephine seeped into the crack of light in the hall, closing the door behind her.

The King had slipped out just as the newly formed detective was snapping back.

Bullock seized his first breath of peace in forever and held it in his chest until the death was absolute and the rattle subsided.

Baby Dagger knocked and entered Nolita's room moments later. The soldier touched the detective's shoulder and led him to the hall.

"I'll take care of this. Go home to your family."

And Bullock did just that.

Nobody ever questioned the odd connection between Josephine and Baby Dagger. They only knew that she was always there when The King needed her and barely a beckon or nod was needed.

“Let's clean it up,” Bee Dee said clapping her hands together. “I'll take care of the heap, you take the floors.”

Nolita had never been happier to tidy up and she'd never felt so clean.

Josephine went to bed and lay on top of the covers. It was a warm night and she didn't feel like undressing. She felt stripped already. Everything was just getting too naked around here.

Chapter 39

Silent Tattle

Josephine lay on top of the cool comforter and turned toward Moonface in his crib. He was snoring softly like his daddy and she stroked his gilded strands, smoothing out the roughness of his breathing. Just like his Da.

She rolled off the bed and padded into Sun Son's room. He was spread across the sheets, all arms and legs, blond hair striping his dark brows. He was always beautiful but tonight he looked like the version of his father whom she'd loved so long ago.

She slipped into the kitchen and looked around. She missed home.

Sitting at the table she stared through the curtains just as Baby Dee's shadow cast itself across the grape-gapped lace. She could hear the drag and thump as her soldier dropped the hump into the bed of her old pickup.

Josephine never knew where the sins ended up and she never asked. Baby Dee had a secret forgetting place and that's where the forgotten lay.

She sighed and closed her eyes as the dust curled up under the fat tires and she waited for some kind of sign, any kind of bellow or whisper that would call her back home.

Her cell buzzed, startling Josephine as it scurried across the cast-iron tabletop like a beetle toward the edge. She grabbed it before it fell, before the clatter could wake the boys.

She heard nothing on the other end and she returned the nothingness.

She listened hard and suddenly recognized the sound of this silence. His silence.

It had a familiar satisfaction and finality to it, a quiet that rang louder than hammered leaded bells.

He'd found her and he was letting her know.

This time Josephine was ready.

Chapter 40

Somebody Waits for You

Josephine was becoming a ghost at The Lost Chambers. She swirled up every now and again, all see-through and soft. Out of the corner of their eyes they would catch her floating down the halls, seeping into walls and doorways as quickly as she appeared.

Baby Dagger had been taking care of the day-to-day without the presence of The King and doing a fine job at that. Josephine was needed less and less and Bee Dee was a natural at the running of the Pennybrides.

Josephine was feeling edgy and exposed since the silent call. She'd sometimes heat with an imagined gaze and when she'd turn around toward the improbable beam, nothing was watching. It was getting unnerving and she kept the boys as close as she could.

She washed, dried, cooked, cleaned and read about all the monsters running free in this new and wildest west and she would get that same sudden rise of responsible blood to her fists. But they stayed clenched and empty. For now, these were not her battles. She remained ready for her own final war.

As she bathed the blond princes that sweltering Saturday night, she heard a scraping on the wall outside, beneath the bathroom window. Her hands froze in the warm soapy water as she pulled the plug. Up and out, dried and dressed the babes were then tucked tightly in their beds.

She remained in her armor and stomped to the living room, closing the door to the hallway behind her. The solid form of The Outlaw King was coming into focus, the weight of the crown sinking her steps further into the wood.

She slid her sharp and pointy down the back of her Levi's and sat stiller than still in the gnarled and nicked rocker, facing the widening crack in the front door.

First a sliver of orange gold streamed in and then the black shadow that would block her sunset this hot and daunting evening entered.

Josephine rose and faced her monster.

He seeped in slowly, an ominous and silent backlit silhouette wearing an outline only Josephine could trace and fill in with all of the remembered details of a day gone very wrong.

He closed the door behind him and stepped into the lamplight so she could see what had become of her creation.

He was thinner then he'd ever been, half of what she made him and he was wearing the weather on his skin. His green eyes set deeper in dark rings and his ashy strands hung way over his thick and dark brows.

Just like Sun Son's eyes, she thought.

He took a step forward and her pale hand found the heated handle of the ender, gripping it easily as if she'd practiced this all of her life.

His left Doc Marten found the only squeaky plank in the room and as it landed it squealed loudly, shrill enough to wake the boys. Josephine glanced at the door to their hallway making sure her eldest boy hadn't stirred.

The Monster. Her monster. He brought down the rest of his seventy-five inches to rest on a perfectly executed kneel, a bow a creature could only conjure for its creator. Josephine cocked her head keeping her eyes on his every move, wondering if this was some new kind of trick he'd learned outside of her realm.

On his knees, The Monster stretched his leather-draped arms out like some kind of sorry, beaten beast and looked up into the eyes of The Outlaw King. She held his gaze for what seemed minutes until hot tears streamed down both of their cheeks.

Without a word he closed his eyes and bowed his head, offering up his guilty pate to its rightful owner to do with what she wished.

Josephine felt the blue eyes peering through the hallway door. She pushed it open with the heel of her boot, never taking her eyes off of the father of her first-born.

Sun Son entered slowly and took his place next to his mother. With her free hand she stroked his hair from his eyes and slipped her arm over his shoulder.

The Monster lifted his face and saw the vision of the two things that formed him, the two beings that ruled his breath, his beat and his bitter end.

Josephine inhaled as deep as it goes and released her grip on the boy. She knew where he needed to go.

He sprang forward and fell into his father's arms, sobbing with laughter.

As The Monster embraced his only child, Josephine brought her hidden hand forward, lifted her chin and spoke the final piece to his puzzle: "Somebody waits for you."

And, of course, somebody still waited for Josephine.

Chapter 41

The Royal Family of the New and Wildest West

Josephine packed the gleaming black Lincoln and got the boys ready for the last few miles of their journey. Baby Dagger was stoic but not too proud to weep at the feet of her King as Josephine slipped the keys and the deeds into the pocket of the woman she had called friend for so long.

As she closed the trunk and buckled the babies, she turned and looked at all the tracks they'd laid out here on the outskirts of her kingdom. She hugged each Pennybride and inhaled the scent of their sweetness one last time before sliding onto the leather bench and taking her legend with her as she sped out into the hot evening sun.

Josephine didn't consult the rearview until they'd hit the asphalt and then that's all she could do: Look at the faces of the reason she came to rule this new world in the first place.

Josephine's heart bulged through her ribs while she steered the borrowed black dragon back to its rightful owner.

She turned up their street and wondered what it would be like to say it out loud, to reveal the shiny new name as the place she lived with her family, the house on the corner with the even numbers tacked to the fresh stucco wall.

The boys were fast asleep by the time she slipped in the driveway. She sat for the longest moment, waiting.

The Saint was washing his single dish and solitary glass, readying himself for another lonely night. He slapped the faucet off and gripped the edges of the counter. He dropped his head and stared down into the black sink she had chosen, the one she had said was "classy" and he laughed in spite of the spike of pain piercing his very soul.

He looked out into the back yard, the one they knew the boys would love, with lots of grass and a play set with a slide and a baby swing. The sun was almost gone and nothing illuminated the street except for oncoming headlights that quivered with acceleration, just like his Lincoln used to do.

Everything stopped as The Saint stared into those headlights. He blinked hard and took a step toward the sliding-glass door. He squinted and evened his sight with the horizon, trying to bring on some form of super-vision, a type of seeing that would reveal what kind of contraption was wrapped around those lights and who was driving it.

As it came closer, he dared admit that it was indeed black and indeed a Lincoln. He started to sweat and shake.

As it passed the house he sprinted to the front door, where he couldn't even begin to hope it was she.

He flung it open and took five steps toward the beast that was indeed his 1964 Lincoln Continental. He froze.

Josephine clicked the chromie and her left boot hit the cement driveway with a clomp. She couldn't take her eyes off of him, his dimpled chin, thick brown hair and chiseled, wide-open expression. Just like Moonface.

She swung the other leg around and stood next to the open door.

He couldn't believe it; there she was, his Josephine, standing in her very own driveway, looking every bit as beautiful as the day they met.

Sun Son awoke with a start and rubbed his eyes with his fists. He saw The Saint and with the unbridled glee of a child ran to him and clung like a spider monkey. The Saint got down on his knees and pressed the boy's face to his chest while the tears ran down both of their cheeks. He kept his eyes on Josephine.

She didn't come toward him. She walked to the back-passenger's suicide door and clicked the handle. He watched as she bent inside for what seemed an eternity.

She unbuckled the sleeping baby boy and lifted him from the carrier. He could see the bundle but again didn't dare to wish.

Sun Son cried, "That's our baby, Da! That's our baby!"

The Saint lifted Sun Son in his arms and carried him over to Josephine who was holding the child. His child! He was not only alive but he was kicking! Moonface awoke and revealed the same baby blues as his brother's and The Saint threw back his head and laughed loud through the river of relief streaming down his face.

He examined the baby's hands and feet, his fat legs and his chubby arms. He looked down on the round face and smiled. Josephine offered the babe to his father and The Saint held his son for the very first time. He kissed him on the forehead and Moonface giggled. Now it was Josephine's turn to laugh.

The Saint grabbed her with his free arm and inhaled the scent that kept his faith after all of these months. He kissed her deep and soft and Josephine melted inside the embrace she'd longed for all of her regal life.

Sun Son ran to the doorway and impatiently yelled for them all to come inside, as though only a moment had passed for the bossy prince.

They entered their stucco palace, the royal family of the new and wildest west, and for the first time in their restless kingdom, a true calm smoothed over the tattered landscape. A new kind of peace covered the weary warriors with warmth they'd hold onto through all the winters to come.

THE END

From the Author

Did you know that there's an accompanying album that goes with this novel?

It's called *Josephine the Outlaw King: the album* and it's by A BROKEHEART PRO (aka, Jeannette Kantzalis).

Sultry, gothic, alt/country, rockabilly moods abound on this 9 song disc, including a fabulously dark version of Kate Bush's, "Running Up That Hill".

You can find it on iTunes, CDBABY.com, Amazon, emusic, anywhere you buy music, available as CD and MP3's.

Still want more?

There's an audiobook version of *Josephine the Outlaw King* as well!

AUDIOBOOK Available on iTunes and
http://josephinetheoutlawking.com

Helpful links:
http://www.abrokeheartpro.com
http://www.josephinetheoutlawking.com
http://facebook.com/josephinetheoutlawking
http://twitter.com/abrokeheartpro

About the Author

Jeannette Louise Kantzalis is an accomplished songwriter/singer/musician born and raised in the working class suburbs of Southern California, aka, the "Inland Empire".

She still lives there with her husband and two sons.

Josephine the Outlaw King is her first novel.

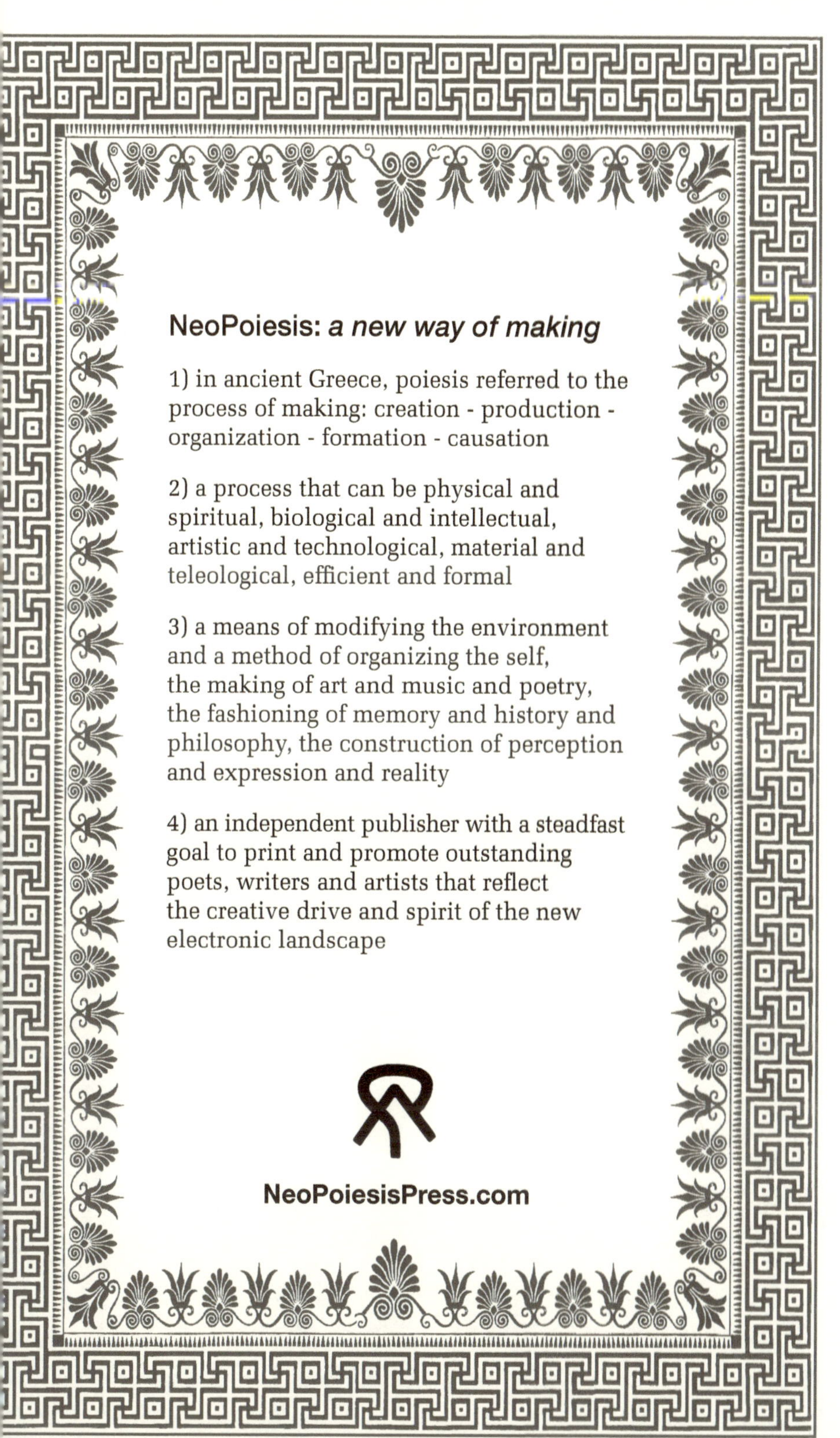

NeoPoiesis: *a new way of making*

1) in ancient Greece, poiesis referred to the process of making: creation - production - organization - formation - causation

2) a process that can be physical and spiritual, biological and intellectual, artistic and technological, material and teleological, efficient and formal

3) a means of modifying the environment and a method of organizing the self, the making of art and music and poetry, the fashioning of memory and history and philosophy, the construction of perception and expression and reality

4) an independent publisher with a steadfast goal to print and promote outstanding poets, writers and artists that reflect the creative drive and spirit of the new electronic landscape

NeoPoiesisPress.com

www.ingramcontent.com/pod-product-compliance
Lightning Source LLC
Chambersburg PA
CBHW030520310726
48979CB00010B/1738/J
* 9 7 8 0 9 8 3 2 7 4 7 6 6 *